## HARLEQUIN® Presents

Welcome to the December 2008 collection of Harlequin Presents!

This month, be sure to read Lynne Graham's *The Greek Tycoon's Disobedient Bride,* the first book in her exciting new trilogy, VIRGIN BRIDES, ARROGANT HUSBANDS. Plus, don't miss the second installment of Sandra Marton's THE SHEIKH TYCOONS series, *The Sheikh's Rebellious Mistress.* Get whisked off into a world of glamour, luxury and passion in Abby Green's *The Mediterranean Billionaire's Blackmail Bargain,* in which innocent Alicia finds herself falling for hard-hearted Dante. Italian tycoon Luca O'Hagan will stop at nothing to make Alice his bride in Kim Lawrence's *The Italian's Secretary Bride,* and in Helen Brooks's *Ruthless Tycoon, Innocent Wife,* virgin Marianne Carr will do anything to save her home, and ruthless Rafe Steed is on hand to help her. Things begin to heat up at the office for interior designer Merrow in Trish Wylie's *His Mistress, His Terms,* when playboy Alex sets out to break all the rules. Independent Cally will have one night she'll never forget with bad-boy billionaire Blake in Natalie Anderson's *Bought: One Night, One Marriage.* And find out if Allie can thaw French doctor Remy de Brizat's heart in Sara Craven's *Bride of Desire.* Happy reading!

We'd love to hear what you think about Presents. E-mail us at Presents@hmb.co.uk or join in the discussions at www.iheartpresents.com and www.sensationalromance.blogspot.com, where you'll also find more information about books and authors!

*Legally wed,*
*but he's never said,*
*"I love you."*
*They're...*

*The series where marriages are made*
*in haste...and love comes later.*

*Look out for more WEDLOCKED!*
*wedding stories, available only from*
*Harlequin Presents®.*

# *Sara Craven*

# BRIDE OF DESIRE

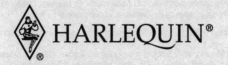

TORONTO • NEW YORK • LONDON
AMSTERDAM • PARIS • SYDNEY • HAMBURG
STOCKHOLM • ATHENS • TOKYO • MILAN • MADRID
PRAGUE • WARSAW • BUDAPEST • AUCKLAND

ISBN-13: 978-0-373-23548-3
ISBN-10:      0-373-23548-8

BRIDE OF DESIRE

First North American Publication 2008.

This edition published by arrangement with Harlequin Books S.A.

® and TM are trademarks of the publisher. Trademarks indicated with ® are registered in the United States Patent and Trademark Office, the Canadian Trade Marks Office and in other countries.

www.eHarlequin.com

**Printed in U.S.A.**

All about the author...
*Sara Craven*

**SARA CRAVEN** was born in South Devon,
England, and grew up in a house by the sea.
After leaving grammar school, she worked as
a local journalist, covering everything from
flower shows to murders. She started writing for
Harlequin Books in 1975.

Sara appeared on the U.K. Channel Four game
show *Fifteen to One,* and in 1997 became U.K.
Television Mastermind of Great Britain. In 2005,
she was a member of the Romantic Novelists'
Association team on *University Challenge—
The Professionals.*

Sara lives near her family in Warwickshire—
Shakespeare country—amid several thousand
books and an amazing video and DVD collection.

When she's not writing, she likes to travel in
Europe, particularly in Italy and Greece. She
loves music, theater, cooking and eating in
good restaurants, but reading will always be her
greatest passion.

# PROLOGUE

IT WAS always the same dream. A long, deserted beach, stretching out into infinity. Straight, firm sand under her bare feet. No twists, no turns. No rocks or other place of concealment anywhere. Near at hand, the hiss and whisper of the sea's rising tide.

And suddenly, behind her, the steady drumming of a horse's hooves, pursuing her. Drawing closer all the time, relentless—inescapable. Preparing to ride her down...

Not daring to look over her shoulder, she began to run, going faster and faster, yet knowing as she did so that there was no escape. That her pursuer would follow her always.

She awoke gasping, sitting bolt upright in the big bed as she stared into the darkness, dry-mouthed, her heart pounding to the point of suffocation and her thin nightdress sticking to her sweat-dampened body.

And then she heard it—the low growl of thunder almost overhead, and the slam of rain against her window. No tidal race or galloping hoof-beats, she recognised shakily. Just a storm in the night—the inevitable climax of the mini-heatwave of the past few days.

She sagged back against the mound of pillows, suppressing a sob.

A dream, she told herself. Triggered by the weather. Nothing more. Only a dream. And one day—one night soon—it would let her go. *He* would let her go. And she would know some peace at last. Surely…

# CHAPTER ONE

As ALLIE came down the broad curving staircase, she paused for a moment to look at the view from the big casement window on the half-landing.

There was nothing new to see. Just the grounds of Marchington Hall in all their formal splendour, unfolding over immaculately kept lawns down to the gleam of the lake in the distance. To her right, she could just glimpse the mellow brick walls of the Fountain Court, while to the left dark green cypresses sheltered the Italian Garden.

But on a day like this, when the air seemed to sparkle after the rain in the night, the vista made her heart lift. It even made her feel that being forced to deal with all the petty restrictions and irritations of life at the Hall might be worth it, after all.

Worth it for Tom's sake anyway, she thought. I have to believe that. I must. Because there is nothing else…

Her throat tightened suddenly, uncontrollably, and she made to turn away. As she did so, she caught sight of her own reflection, and paused again. She looked like a ghost, she thought soberly. A pale, hollow-eyed, fair-haired phantom, without life or substance. And as tense as if she was stretched on wire.

Part of that, of course, was down to last night's storm. Part, but not all.

Because it also had to do with the ongðing battle over the upbringing of her fourteen-month-old son, which, in spite of her best efforts, seemed to be turning into a war of attrition.

She'd just been to visit him in his nursery, to make sure that he hadn't been woken by the thunder, but had been faced by the usual confrontation with Nanny, looking disapproving over this disruption to Tom's routine.

'He's having his breakfast, Lady Marchington.'

'I'm aware of that,' Allie had returned, counting to ten under her breath. 'In fact, I'd like to help feed him. I've said so many times.'

'We prefer to have as few distractions at mealtimes as possible,' Nanny returned with regal finality.

And if I had the guts of a worm, Allie thought grimly, I'd stand up to the boot-faced old bag.

But behind Nanny's portly and commanding frame, she knew, stood the outwardly frail figure of Grace, the Dowager Lady Marchington, her mother-in-law, known irreverently in the village as the Tungsten Tartar.

Any overt clash with Nanny led straight to 'an atmosphere' in the nursery, and also resulted in Allie becoming the target of the elder Lady Marchington's icy displeasure. An experience to be avoided.

Anything for a quiet life, she'd told herself as she'd

left the nursery, closing the door behind her. And, my God, was this ever a quiet life.

She supposed that for Tom's sake she wouldn't have it any other way. He was Hugo's heir, she reminded herself stonily, so she should have known what to expect.

Besides, on the surface at least, the Hall had all the necessary elements to supply him with an idyllic childhood.

But I'd just like to be able to enjoy it with him, she thought rebelliously. Without Nanny standing guard as if I was a potential kidnapper instead of his mother.

He said his first word to her, not me. And it wasn't Mama either, which hurt. And I missed the moment he took his first step, too. It's as if I don't feature in the scheme of things at all. I gave him birth, and now I'm being sidelined. It's a ludicrous situation to be in.

Most of her friends were young marrieds, struggling to cope with child-rearing alongside the demands of their careers. They must think that, apart from the tragedy of being widowed at twenty-one, she'd pretty much fallen on her feet.

After all, she had a large house to live in, a staff to run it, and no money or childcare problems.

Besides, some of them clearly thought that the premature end of her marriage was a blessing in disguise too, although they never said so openly.

And if they did, Allie thought, sighing, could I really deny it?

She walked slowly across the hall and, drawing a deep breath, entered the dining room. Grace Marchington was seated at the head of the table—although 'enthroned' might be a better description, Allie thought as she fielded the disparaging glance aimed at her denim skirt and white cheesecloth blouse, closely followed, as usual, by the glance at the watch—just pointed enough to be noticeable.

'Good morning, Alice. Did you sleep well?' She didn't wait for an answer, but picked up the small brass bell beside her place and rang it sharply. 'I'll ask Mrs Windom to bring some fresh toast.'

Allie took her seat and poured herself some coffee. 'I'm sorry if I'm late. I popped in to see Tom on my way down.'

'Not a terribly convenient time, my dear, as I think Nanny has mentioned to you.'

'Oh, yes,' Allie said. 'She has.' She fortified herself with some coffee. 'So, perhaps she could suggest when it would be more appropriate for me to visit my own son. Because somehow I always seem to get it wrong.'

Lady Marchington replaced her cup in its saucer in a measured way. 'I'm not sure I understand you, Alice.'

Allie took a breath. 'I'd like to see Tom first thing in the morning without it being regarded as an unreasonable request. In fact, I'd love to be there when he wakes up, so that I can sort out his clothes and bath him, and then give him his breakfast. That's surely not too much to ask.'

'Are you implying that Nanny is incapable in some way of supplying Tom's needs? May I remind you that she was entrusted with the care of Hugo as soon as he was born.'

'I do realise that, yes,' Allie said wearily. *I've never been allowed to forget it.*

'And I'm sure you also recall that there was a time, after Tom's birth, when Nanny's presence became indispensable?'

*The dagger between the ribs...*

'Yes, I had postnatal depression for a while.' Allie kept her tone even. 'But I got over it.'

'Did you, my dear? Sometimes I wonder.' Her mother-in-law gave her a sad smile. 'Of course, you are still grieving for our beloved boy, which may account for the mood swings I sometimes detect. But I'm sure Dr Lennard would be happy to recommend someone—a specialist who could help you over this difficult period in your life.'

Allie's lips tightened. 'You think that wanting to look after my small child means I need a psychiatrist?'

Lady Marchington looked almost shocked. 'There are many different levels of therapy, Alice. And it was only a suggestion, after all.'

As if signifying that the matter was closed, she turned her attention to the pile of post which had been placed beside her, as it was every morning. And, as she did so, Allie suddenly spotted the pale blue envelope with the French stamp, halfway down, and stifled a small gasp.

A letter from Tante Madelon, she thought, and felt the hair stand up on the back of her neck. Was that the real reason for last night's dream, and not the storm at all? Why she'd heard all over again the sibilant rush of the incoming tide and the thunder of the pursuing hoofbeats? Because somehow she'd sensed that all the memories of Brittany she'd tried so hard to bury were about to be revived?

Her heart was thumping against her ribs, but she knew there was no point in claiming the letter. That wasn't the way the system worked. All the mail delivered to the Hall came to Grace first, to be scrutinised before it was handed out to staff and family alike.

And if she thought you were taking an undue interest in any item, she was quite capable of taking the day's post to her private sitting room and letting you seethe quietly for half a day, or even twenty-four hours, before handing it over with the mellifluous words, 'I think this must be for you.'

'It's madness,' Allie had once told Hugo heatedly. 'Your mother is the ultimate control freak. Why don't you say something?'

But he'd only looked at her, brows raised in haughty surprise. 'Mother's always dealt with the mail. My father preferred it, and I don't see it as a problem.'

But then Hugo had seen very little as a problem, apart from the utter necessity of providing a son and heir for his beloved estate. That, in the end, had been the driving force—the obsession in his ruined life. Two ruined lives, if she counted her own, and she tried hard not to do that. Bitterness, after all, was futile, and damaged no one but herself. Regret, too, altered nothing.

But was she still mourning her late husband, as her

mother-in-law had suggested? In her innermost heart, she doubted that. The suddenness of his death had certainly been an acute shock, but she suspected her reaction was largely triggered by guilt because she'd never really loved him.

For a long time she'd felt numb—too emotionally paralysed even to feel relief that the nightmare of their marriage had ended—but that had been over and done with long ago.

Slowly and carefully, she'd begun to find herself again, and somehow she had to move on from that— to regain the here and now, and stop allowing Grace to treat her as some kind of cipher—even if it did end with blood on the carpet.

How to go about it, of course, was not so clear, she told herself ironically. Because her mother-in-law seemed to hold all the winning cards.

In those tragic crowded weeks after Hugo had died with such shocking suddenness and Tom had been born, Allie herself had temporarily descended into some bleak, dark limbo.

It was then that Grace Marchington had effortlessly reassumed the role of mistress of the house. In fact, Allie could see, looking back, that she'd never really been away.

I was just the temporary usurper who gave Hugo the son he'd craved, she thought. And after that I was supposed to retire into well-deserved obscurity, while Grace and Nanny pursued the task of turning Tom into a tintype of Marchington Man.

But that's not going to happen, because I won't let it.

She realised, however, that she needed to conserve her energies for the battles she had to win—and Grace being anally retentive over a bunch of letters was not the most important. A minor irritation at best.

So, for the time being, she sat and ate the toast that Mrs Windom had brought, and never gave a second glance at the mail that Grace was examining with such torturous slowness. It might only be a small victory, but it counted.

She looked instead at the picture on the wall in front of her. It was a portrait of Hugo that his mother had commissioned for his twenty-fifth birthday, two years before the accident. Lady Marchington had not been altogether satisfied with the result, saying it was a poor likeness. But Allie wasn't so sure about that. The artist had given Hugo credit for his undoubted good looks, but also hinted at a slight fleshiness about the jaw, and a peevish line to the mouth. Nor had he made any attempt to conceal that the crisply cut dark hair was already beginning to recede.

It was Hugo, she thought, as he would have become if his life had taken a different path. If there'd been more time…

And suddenly superimposed on it, she realised, her heart bumping, was another face—thinner, swarthier, with a beak of a nose and heavy-lidded eyes, as blue and cold as the sea. And a voice in her head whispered a name that she'd tried hard to forget—*Remy*…

'This seems to be yours, Alice.'

She started violently as she realised that Lady Marchington, lips faintly pursed, was holding out the blue envelope.

'I presume it's from your French great-aunt,' the older woman added. 'I hope it isn't bad news.'

'I hope so too,' Allie said lightly, ignoring the hint that she should open it instantly and divulge the contents. 'But at least she's alive.'

She heard the hiss of indrawn breath, and braced herself for a chilling rebuke over inappropriate levity, but instead the dining room door opened to admit the housekeeper.

'Excuse me, your ladyship, but Mrs Farlow is asking to speak to you on the telephone. A problem with the Garden Club accounts.'

'I'll come.' Lady Marchington rose with an expression on her face that boded ill for the unfortunate Club treasurer. And for Allie, too, if she was still around when her mother-in-law returned.

As soon as she was alone, Allie went quickly across to the French windows and let herself out on to the terrace. A few minutes later she was pushing open the wrought-iron gate into the Fountain Court. It was one of her favourite places, with its gravelled paths, the raised beds planted with roses, just coming into flower, and the tall, cascading centrepiece of ferocious tritons and swooning nymphs from which it took its name.

It was an odd thing to find at an English country house, she had to admit, but it had been designed and installed by a much earlier Sir Hugo, who'd fallen in

love with Italy while on the Grand Tour, and had
wanted a permanent memento of his travels.

Allie loved the fountain for its sheer exuberance,
and for the cool, soothing splash of its water which
made even the hottest day seem restful. She sat on one
of the stone benches and opened Tante's letter. She
read it through swiftly, then, frowning, went back to
the beginning, absorbing its contents with greater care.

It was not, in fact, good news. The writing was
wavery, and not always easy to decipher, but the gist
of it was that all was far from well with her great-aunt.

It seems that this will be my last summer at Les
Sables d'Ignac. However, I have had a good life
here, and I regret only that so long has passed
since we were together. You remind me so much
of my beloved sister, and it would make me truly
happy to see you again, my dearest child. I hope
with all my heart that you can spare me a little
time from your busy life to visit me. Please, my
dear Alys, come to me, and bring your little boy
with you also. As he is the last of the Vaillac
blood, I so long to see him.

My God, Allie thought, appalled. What on earth
could be wrong with her? Tante Madelon had always
given the impression that she was in the most robust
of health. But then she hadn't seen her for almost two
years—and that was indeed a long time.

She realised, of course, that her great-aunt must be

in her late seventies, although her looks and vigour had always belied her age. In fact, to Allie she'd always seemed immortal, only the silvering of her hair marking the inevitable passage of time.

Soberly, she thought of Tante as she'd seen her last. The older woman's pointed face had been drawn and anxious, but the dark, vivid eyes had still been full of life. Full of love for this girl, her only living relative.

'Don't go back, *ma chérie*,' she'd urged. 'There is nothing for you there. Stay here with me…' Her voice had died away, leaving other things unsaid.

And Allie had replied, stumbling over the words, her head reeling, her emotions in shreds, 'I—can't.'

Now, she took a deep breath to calm herself, then slowly re-read the postscript at the end, the words running down the page as if the writer had been almost too weary to hold the pen.

Alys, I promise there is nothing that should keep you away, and that you have no reason to fear such a visit.

In plain words, Tante was offering her assurance— the essential guarantee that she thought Allie would want. Telling her, in effect, that Remy de Brizat would not be there. That he was still working abroad with his medical charity.

Only it wasn't as simple as that. It wasn't enough. He might not be physically present, but Allie knew that her memory—her senses—would find him everywhere.

That she'd see him waiting on the shore, or find his face carved into one of the tall stone megaliths that dotted the headland. That she'd feel him in every grain of sand or blade of grass. That she'd hear his laughter on the wind, and his voice in the murmur of the sea.

And, in the fury of the storm, she would relive the anger and bitterness of their parting, she thought, as she'd done last night. And she shivered in spite of the warmth of the morning.

Besides, she had too many memories already.

Her breathing quickened suddenly to pain. Words danced off the page at her. *Please, my dear Alys, come to me…*

She closed her eyes to block them out, and heard herself repeat aloud—'I can't.'

Then she crushed the letter in her hand, and pushed it into the pocket of her skirt.

She got to her feet and began to wander restlessly down the gravelled walk, forcing herself to think about other things—other people. To build a wall against those other memories.

Turning her thoughts determinedly to the Vaillac sisters, Celine and Madelon. During the Second World War, their family had sheltered her grandfather, Guy Colville, an airman forced to bail out on his way home. He'd broken his leg during his parachute descent, but had managed to crawl to a nearby barn, where Celine Vaillac had found him.

The Vaillacs had nursed him back to health, and risked their lives to keep him hidden and fed, eventually enabling him to be smuggled north to the Channel coast and back to England in a fishing boat. It was part of family folklore, and a story she'd never tired of hearing when she was a child.

She thought how romantic it was that Guy had never forgotten the pretty, shyly smiling Celine, and how, as soon as the war ended, he'd returned to their rambling farmhouse with his younger brother Rupert, to make sure that she and her family had all survived relatively unscathed, and discover whether Celine shared similar memories of their time together.

That first visit had been followed by others, and, to Guy's surprise, Rupert had insisted on going with him each time. When eventually Guy had proposed to Celine, and been accepted, his brother had confessed that he too had fallen in love with her younger sister, Madelon, a vivacious imp of a girl, and suggested a double wedding.

It was a real fairy-tale, Allie thought wistfully, but the happy ending had been short-lived—for her grandparents at least. Celine had always been the fairer of the two, and the quieter. A girl slender as a lily and ultimately as delicate. Because what should have been the straightforward birth of her first child had developed unexpected and severe complications which, tragically, she had not survived.

Guy had been totally devastated, firstly by the loss of his adored wife, and by having to learn to cope with a newborn motherless son. He had naturally turned to Rupert and Madelon, who'd provided him with the deep, steadfast support he needed, in spite of their own grief. Ironically, they themselves had remained childless, pouring their affection and care into the up-bringing of their nephew, forming unbroken ties into Paul Colville's adult life.

So, Tante had been an important part of Allie's back-ground from the moment she was born. It had only been when both Guy and her husband had died that she'd finally decided to return to Brittany, renting a house in Quimper for a while. Allie and her father Paul had visited her there on several occasions, although her mother had never accompanied them, making the excuse that she was a poor sailor, who found the ferry crossing a nightmare.

Looking back, Allie always suspected that Fay Colville had resented her husband's deep affection for his French aunt, and that it had been jealousy rather than *mal de mer* that kept her in England. She'd also openly disliked the fact that Allie had been chris-tened Alys, rather than the Anglicised Alice that she herself always used.

Fay had become a widow herself by the time Tante had found herself a cottage by the sea in place of the family farm, which had been sold long ago, and was now a complex of *gîtes*. Even then, she had rejected each and every offer of hospitality from Madelon Colville, but she'd objected almost hysterically when Allie had sug-gested she should visit her great-aunt by herself.

'Are you mad?' she'd stormed. 'What will Hugo think?'

Allie lifted her chin. 'Does that matter?'

'Oh, don't talk like a fool.' Fay glared at her. 'You don't seem to have a clue how to keep a young man interested.'

'Perhaps because I suspect it's only a passing interest,' Allie told her coolly.

'Nonsense. He's taken you down to the Hall, hasn't he? Introduced you to his mother?'

'Yes,' Allie agreed reluctantly.

'Well, the invitation must be a sign that she approves of Hugo's choice.'

'And what about my own views on Hugo's choice? Supposing I don't approve?'

'That,' her mother said sharply, 'is not funny.'

But I, thought Allie, wasn't joking.

Her attitude to Hugo Marchington had always been ambivalent. At first she'd been convinced she was falling in love, carried away by the sheer glamour of him. She'd frankly enjoyed dining in top restaurants, being whisked off to polo matches, race meetings, regattas, and all the other leading events in the social calendar.

But, as weeks had become months, she'd realised that she simply did not know her own mind. And if he was indeed planning to ask her to become engaged to him, as she'd suspected, she had no real idea of what answer to give him. Which, by then, she should have done.

Naturally, she'd been flattered. Who wouldn't have been? In previous eras Hugo would have been considered the catch of the county, because he was rich, handsome, and he could be charming.

Yes, she thought. That was the sticking point. Could be—but wasn't always. In fact he'd sometimes revealed the makings of a nasty temper, although he had invariably been contrite afterwards.

And, in spite of all the assiduous attention he'd paid her, she hadn't been altogether convinced that his heart was in it. He might, in fact, have been behaving as he was expected to do.

At the beginning of their relationship he'd made a couple of serious attempts at seduction, which Allie had fended off just as seriously. He hadn't repelled her physically—but nor had he stirred her blood to the point of surrender. His kisses had never made her long for more. But she'd been aware that could have been due to an element of emotional reserve within herself, which, in turn, gave her an aura of coolness that some men might find a challenge.

At any rate, she'd known that giving herself in the ultimate intimacy would have implied a level of commitment that she had simply not been prepared for. Or not with Hugo Marchington—not yet. Although she had supposed that might change eventually.

In view of her lukewarm attitude, she'd been genuinely surprised when, instead of writing her off as a lost cause sexually, and looking for a more willing partner, he'd continued to ask her out.

I wonder, she'd thought, if his mother's told him it's time he settled down, and I'm handy and reasonably presentable, but not so devastating that I'll ever outshine him.

Having met Lady Marchington, she had quite believed it. She had also believed that she genuinely ticked enough of the right boxes to be acceptable. And her mother's Knightsbridge address would have raised no eyebrows either.

All the same, in her lunch hours at the private library where she'd worked as an assistant, she had found herself scanning the job columns for work that would take her away from London.

Maybe I should have obeyed my instincts and moved. Even gone back to college, perhaps, and improved my qualifications. And somehow persuaded my mother that it would be a good thing.

But if I had there would have been no Tom, and, in spite of everything, the thought of him not being here—never having been born—is too awful to contemplate.

Allie brought her restless wanderings to a halt, and gazed around her, assimilating once again the full baroque splendours of the Fountain Court.

I love it, she told herself wryly. But I don't belong here. I never did. The Hall is not my home, but it has to be Tom's. Some good has to come out of all this unhappiness.

He belongs here. I made that decision, and I have to remain for his sake.

But I have to find something to do with my own life. I'm edgy all the time because I feel confined at the Hall—claustrophobic. I have no actual role to play, so I spend my days just—hanging around. It's boring, and it's not healthy either.

And I won't think of the life I might have had if I'd done as Tante Madelon begged and stayed in Brittany, because that was never an actual possibility—always just a dream. And a dangerous dream at that.

Because, once again, she realised, there was a sound echoing in her head—the sure, steady beat of a horse's hooves coming behind her, just as she'd heard them so many times over the past months, sleeping and waking. Following her—getting closer all the time.

She said aloud, 'It's just my imagination playing tricks, nothing else. Imagination—and more guilt.'

She went slowly back to her bench, her great-aunt's letter like a lead weight in her pocket, and sat down. Although all she really wanted to do was put her hands over her ears and run.

But I've already done that—twice, she thought, her throat closing. And now, God help me, I have to live with the consequences.

All of them…

And if that means facing up to my memories, and exorcising them for ever, then so be it.

# CHAPTER TWO

SHE'D fainted, she remembered, sliding from her chair at the breakfast table one morning under Grace's astonished eye. That was how it had all begun. And it hadn't been the family's usual doctor who'd answered the summons to attend her ladyship, but a locum, young, brisk, and totally unimpressed by his surroundings.

He'd insisted on seeing Allie alone, questioning her with real kindness, and eventually she'd realised he was suggesting she might be pregnant. And suddenly she'd found herself crying, and unable to stop, as she told him how utterly impossible that was, or ever could be. And of the constant pressure she'd been under during her four months of soulless marriage, both from Hugo and his mother, to somehow bring about a miracle and give him the child he craved.

'He doesn't believe any of the consultants.' Her voice had choked on a sob. 'He says it's my fault. But I don't know what to do. I don't know what he *expects* me to do.'

Confronting Hugo and Grace, the doctor had announced that Lady Marchington had been under a great deal of stress since the wedding, and was in dire need of a complete break, well away from the Hall and its environs.

'A holiday,' Grace had pondered aloud. 'Somewhere in the sun, perhaps, where they have good facilities for wheelchairs.' She gave the interloper an icy smile. 'It is, after all, my son who has suffered the real trauma here.'

'I'm afraid I haven't made myself clear.' The doctor was a stocky man, with sandy hair and a pugnacious expression with a built-in ice deflector. 'Lady Marchington actually needs to get away from all that. Build up her resources. Surely she has friends or family she could go to—somewhere she could relax in undemanding company for a while?'

'I have a very dear great-aunt in Brittany,' Allie said quietly, looking back at him, aware of Grace's barely suppressed fury at the word 'undemanding'. She drew a breath. 'She would have me to stay with her, I know.'

'Ideal.' He nodded. 'Walks on the beach, congenial surroundings, platters of *fruits de mer*, and plenty of sleep. That's what I prescribe. Worth a ton of tranquillisers or sleeping pills.'

'You may as well go,' Hugo told her bitingly after the doctor's departure. 'God knows you're of little use here.'

'And perhaps while you're away,' Grace added with steely annoyance, 'you can consider what you owe to the Marchington name, and come back in a more amenable frame of mind to attend to your duties as Hugo's wife.'

But I'm not his wife. The words screamed in Allie's brain. Because he's not physically capable of being my husband. We all know this, so why must we go on with this terrible pretence? Why do I have to lie beside him in bed, being punished by his anger for something that isn't anyone's fault—just a tragic reality.

She wanted to cry again, but this time with the sheer relief of knowing that she was going to escape it all— just for a little while, although eventually she would have to come back…

'Dearest girl, you look like a ghost,' was her great-aunt's concerned greeting on her arrival at Les Sables d'Ignac. 'And there are deep shadows under your eyes. Are you not sleeping?'

'Well, Hugo does tend to be a little restless. And life has been pretty hectic since the wedding.' She managed a laugh. 'I seem to be public property. People want me to join committees—open things. And Hugo's mother is so much better at that kind of stuff. It all gets—a bit much sometimes.'

There was pause, then Tante said gently, 'I see.'

But please don't see too much, Allie begged under her breath. Or ask questions that I can't answer.

The house was just as she'd remembered, its living room occupying the entire ground floor, where a comfortable sitting area, with two large sofas, flanked a fireplace with a wood-burning stove and was divided from the kitchen area at the far end by a large dining table, covered in oilcloth and surrounded by four high-backed chairs.

She found herself chatting almost feverishly during the evening meal, describing Marchington Hall itself, and its history, recounting anecdotes about some of Hugo's most interesting ancestors, while Tante listened, delicate brows slightly lifted, sometimes offering a faint smile, but more often not. She made her own polite enquiries about Fay's health, and Hugo's progress, accepting the halting replies without further comment.

And when the meal was over, she announced quietly but firmly that Allie should have an early night, and shooed her upstairs. The window in her room was open, its shutters folded back, so that the filmy drapes moved in the breeze from the sea. Allie could hear the splash and hiss of the tide, the rhythm of its ebb and flow producing a faintly soporific effect.

She undressed swiftly, and put on her cotton night-dress. Her final act was to remove her wedding ring and place it in the drawer of the bedside cabinet.

Alice, Lady Marchington, belonged in England, she told herself. Here, for these few precious weeks, she was going to be Alys again. She would live entirely in the present, closing her mind against the recent past and forbidding herself to contemplate the future, although she was aware there were decisions that would have to be made. But somehow—*somehow*—she would build up the strength to do what she had to do in order to survive.

She slid under the crisp white covers of the bed, stretching luxuriously, rediscovering the pleasures of space and privacy, guiltily grateful not to encounter Hugo's bulk beside her. And not to be made to endure the frustration of his fruitless, angry demands.

She fell asleep almost at once, and woke to the pale, sunlit sky of early morning. The wind had freshened in the night, and beyond the cliff-edge the waves were tipped with white. She could taste the salt in the air, and felt her heart lift.

She showered swiftly, dressing in cut-off grey linen pants with a white shirt knotted at the waist, thrust her feet into red canvas shoes, and made her way noiselessly out of the house.

A walk, she thought, to make sure she was properly awake, and then she'd drive into Ignac and pick up the bread and some breakfast croissants at the *boulangerie*.

The bay immediately below the house was a wide crescent of pale sand, backed by a jumble of rocks and boulders and reached by a scramble of narrow steps hewn out of the stone of the cliff-face. It wasn't the easiest access in the world, which helped maintain the bay's privacy—the holidaymaking crowds in this part of Finistere preferring beaches that were more readily available.

Allie had never chosen to bathe here on her visits. She was not a strong swimmer, and was wary about getting out of her depth because of the strong off-shore currents.

Now, she picked her way across the pebbles, then slipped off her shoes, tucking one into each pocket when she reached the sand.

The wind whipped at her hair, sending it streaming across her face, and she laughed aloud and began to run. 'I feel free,' she shouted at a surprised gull, and performed a series of improvised pirouettes, leaping into the air. 'Wonderfully, gorgeously free.'

And, as she did so, she heard the drumming of hooves not far behind her. She turned swiftly and saw a powerful chestnut horse approaching fast along the beach. On its back was a man, hatless, his dark hair dishevelled, wearing riding breeches and a crimson polo shirt.

Allie stepped backwards, realising with vexation that he must have heard her bellowing at the sky, and seen her whirling about like some poor man's dervish. As he passed, she caught a glimpse of swarthy skin in need of a shave, and an impatient sideways glance from eyes as coldly blue as the sea itself.

He called something to her, but his words were carried away by the wind, and she nodded, lifting a hand, pretending that she'd heard. Probably making some sarcastic comment on her dancing, she thought.

He's going in that direction, she noted mentally, as horse and rider disappeared round the curve of the cliff into the next bay. So—I'll go the other way.

She turned, and began to wander in the opposite direction, picking up shells as she went, eventually reaching another cove, narrower than the one she'd left, and sheltered by the steepness of the cliff.

Allie found a flat boulder and sat down, with her back to the wind, aimlessly shifting her shells into various patterns, and wishing that her life could be so easily rearranged. The question she had to ask herself was—how long could she go on living with Hugo? Especially when being treated as some kind of scapegoat in this ludicrous pretence of a marriage.

She'd been emotionally blackmailed into becoming his wife, standing beside his hospital bed as he begged her not to leave him. Told her that he needed her—depended on her.

Manoeuvred and manipulated by his mother, and hers, too, she hadn't known which way to turn. Had been warned that she could be risking his chance of recovery if she walked away. Except there *was* no chance, and everyone knew it. Especially the medical staff.

So I let them convince me, she thought drearily. Told myself I was necessary to him, and, even if I didn't love him, I told myself I could at least have compassion for all that strength and vigour, destroyed for ever by a stupid collision on a polo field. That I couldn't—let him down.

At the time, she reflected bitterly, it had seemed—easier. But how wrong she'd been.

Shuddering violently, Allie swept the shells off the rock into oblivion, almost wishing that she could go with them. Because there was no pattern to her life, and no solution either. Just endurance. Because, however unhappy she might be, Hugo was in a wheelchair, requiring permanent nursing, and she still couldn't abandon him. She'd have to go back.

But she would at least make the most of this all too

brief release. She glanced at her watch, realising it was time she was getting back to the house. She was getting hungry, and besides, Tante would be wondering where she was.

She jumped down from her rock and turned, her hand going to her mouth, stifling a cry. While she'd been sitting there, daydreaming, the sea had been coming in—not gently, but in a strong, steady rush, as she knew it sometimes did along this coast. Tante had warned her about it in the past, insisting that anyone staying at the house must always check the tides before using the beach.

*But I didn't. I didn't give it a moment's thought. I assumed it was on the ebb...*

She looked at the waves, already encroaching at each end of the cove, cutting off her retreat whichever way she turned, and felt sick with fear. There was seaweed on the boulders behind her too, indicating how far the sea could reach.

Oh, God, she thought, I must do something. I can't just stand here, watching the water level rise.

She realised she might have to swim for it, although she knew she'd be struggling even if the sea was like a millpond. On the other hand, if she wasted any more time, she risked being washed against the jut of the overhanging cliff, she realised, swallowing a sob in her throat.

Then, suddenly, there was rescue.

The horse seemed to come from nowhere, eyes rolling, head tossing as it galloped through the waves, urged on by its rider. As they reached the strip of sand where Allie stood, transfixed, the man leaned down, hand extended, spitting an instruction at her in a voice molten with fury.

She set a foot in the stirrup that he had kicked free, and found herself dragged up in front of him, left hanging across the saddle, with her head dangling ignominiously, his hand holding her firmly in place by the waistband of her trousers.

She felt the horse bound forward, and then there was water all around them, the salt spray invading her eyes and mouth, soaking the drift of her hair, chilling the fingers that were gripping the girth until they were numb.

She could feel the fear in the chestnut's bunched muscles—sense the anger in the air from its rider—although he was talking constantly to his mount, his voice quiet and reassuring.

She was scared and aching, every bone in her body shaken as the horse plunged on. She closed her eyes against the dizziness induced by this headlong dash, praying that he would not stumble. That the drag of the sea would not defeat him.

She never knew the exact moment when the almost violent splashing of the water stopped, but when she next dared to look down, she found herself staring at sand, and the beginnings of a rough track leading upwards.

Then the horse was being pulled up, and her rescuer's hold on her was suddenly released. She raised a dazed head, realising that he was dismounting, and then she herself was summarily pulled down from the saddle, without gentleness, and dumped on the stones.

She sank to the ground, coughing and trying to catch her breath. She felt sick and giddy from that nightmare ride, aware too that her clothes were sodden, and her hair hanging in rats' tails.

She looked up miserably, tried to speak and failed, silenced by the scorching fury in the blue eyes, and the battery of fast, enraged French that was being launched at her without mercy.

As he paused to draw breath at last, she said in her schoolgirl's version of the same language. 'I'm sorry. I don't understand.' Then she put her face in her hands and burst into tears.

He swore murderously. She could interpret that at least. Then there was a taut silence, and a clean, if damp, handkerchief was thrust between her fingers.

'You are English?' He spoke more quietly, using her language, his voice clipped, the accent good.

She nodded, still not trusting her voice.

*'Mon Dieu.'* He shook his head. 'Yet you come here to a dangerous shore—alone, and at such an hour, to stroll as if you were in a London park? Are you quite insane?'

She lifted her head. Looked up at him as he stood, soothing his horse with a paradoxically gentle hand.

He was slightly younger than she'd thought, probably in his early thirties, but no friendlier for that. She assimilated a beak of a nose, a formidable chin with a cleft, and a strong mouth with a sensual curve to its lower lip. And his eyes were truly amazing—a colour between azure and turquoise, fringed by long lashes. And brilliant now with the temper he was trying to control. But more, she thought, for the horse's sake than hers.

She said huskily, 'I should have been more careful, I know. But I was thinking about—something else.'

He gestured impatiently. 'But I warned you to go back. Why did you ignore me?'

'I—didn't hear what you said—not properly.'

He muttered something else under his breath. 'You are no doubt accustomed to people shouting at you,' he added contemptuously. 'And have learned to disregard it.'

Allie sank her teeth into her lower lip. Yes, she thought, but not in the way you imagine.

'Again, I'm sorry.' She wiped her face with the handkerchief, detecting a faint fragrance of some masculine cologne in its folds.

'I did not believe it when I looked down from the top of the cliff and saw you there in the Cauldron,' he said harshly. 'We call it that because when the tide is full the water seems to boil over the rocks.'

Allie shuddered. 'I didn't know. I—I've never gone that way before.' *And I wouldn't have done so this time if I hadn't been trying to avoid you...*

'I was almost tempted to leave you,' he went on. 'Instead of risking my life, and my even more valuable horse, to come to the aid of a stranger and a fool.'

She lifted her chin. 'Oh, don't spare me. Please say

exactly what you think,' she invited, with a trace of her usual spirit.

'I shall,' he told her brusquely. He added, 'Roland, you understand, does not care for the sea.'

*Then perhaps you should have left me. It would have been one answer to my problems...*

The thought ran like lightning through her head, but was instantly dismissed as she contemplated the shock and grief that Tante would have suffered if the sea had indeed taken her.

Besides, when faced with it, oblivion had not seemed nearly so desirable, and she knew she would have fought to survive.

She swallowed. 'Then Roland's a true hero.' She got slowly to her feet. 'And—thank you for having second thoughts,' she added with difficulty. She smoothed her hands down her wet trousers, and stopped as a sudden realisation dawned. 'Oh, God, I've lost my shoes. They were in my pockets.'

'I hope you do not expect me to go back for them,' he said with asperity.

'Oh, no,' Allie returned, almost poisonously sweet. 'I think saving my life places me under quite enough obligation to you for one day.'

'Or perhaps not,' he said slowly. 'Where are you staying, *mademoiselle*?'

For a moment, this form of address threw her. Then she remembered her discarded wedding ring. He would naturally assume she was single, and she should put him right instantly. But...

'Why?' she asked, still edgy. 'Are you hoping to be rewarded for bringing back the stray?'

The firm mouth curled. 'You mean there are people who would pay to have you returned to them? *Incroyable*. However, I hope it is not too far,' he added smoothly. 'It could be an uncomfortable journey in bare feet.' He watched the variety of expressions that flitted across her face with an appreciation he did not bother to disguise. 'Or would you prefer to ride back to your accommodation on Roland?'

Neither, she thought. I'd much rather the past hour had never happened. I wish I was back in my room at Les Sables, turning over to sleep again.

'Please make up your mind, *mademoiselle*.' He glanced at his watch. 'I am not a tourist. Unlike you, I have work to go to.'

One day, she promised herself. One day, I'll think of something to say that will wipe that smirk out of your voice.

Except that presupposed they would meet again, which was the last thing she wanted—to keep running into a man who regarded her as a bedraggled idiot.

She lifted her chin. 'Thank you,' she said. 'I think I'd better accept your offer. As long as Roland has forgiven me for his unexpected dip.'

'He has a nature of the most amiable.' He cupped his hands. 'Put your foot here,' he directed, and as she nervously complied he tossed her up into the saddle as if she were thistledown, then began to lead Roland up the slope. 'You had better tell him where he is to take you,' he added over his shoulder.

She said unhappily, 'I'm staying with Madame Colville at Les Sables.' She could just imagine Tante's reaction when she turned up, barefoot on the back of a strange horse, looking like a piece of sub-human flotsam. She added unwillingly, 'I'm her great-niece.'

'Ah,' he said. 'I did not know she had such a relation. But then she is my father's patient, not mine.'

She frowned. 'Patient? You mean you're a doctor?'

'You find it hard to believe? Yet I assure you it is true,' he said. He made a slight inclination of the head. 'Remy de Brizat at your service.'

As she hesitated, he added, 'Now you are supposed to tell me your name, *mademoiselle*. Or is it a secret?'

Not a secret, she thought. But not the whole truth either, which is very wrong of me. But perhaps this is my morning for behaving badly. And anyway, we're unlikely to meet again, so what harm can it really do?

She said, quietly and clearly, 'I'm called Alys, *monsieur*. Alys—Colville.'

'Alys,' he said reflectively. 'A charming name— and French too.'

She wrinkled her nose. 'In England, I'm plain Alice.'

At the top of the slope, he halted Roland and stood looking up at her, his smile faintly twisted. 'You are wrong,' he said softly. 'You could not ever be plain—anything.'

There was an odd, tingling silence, then he added

briskly, 'Now, move back a little, Alys, if you please, so that Roland can take us both.'

She did as she was told, feeling awkward, and hoping the exertion would explain the sudden surge of colour in her face. Remy de Brizat mounted lithely in front of her.

'Hold on to me,' he instructed. 'The medical centre in Ignac opens in one hour, and I must be there.'

Reluctantly, she put her hands on her companion's shoulders, then, as the big horse moved off, she found herself being thrown forward, and hastily clasped her arms round his waist instead.

'*Ça va?*' he queried over his shoulder, as Roland's stride lengthened into a canter.

'I think so,' Allie gasped, clinging on for grim death, and heard him laugh softly.

It wasn't really that far, she realised, as the grey stones of Tante's house came into view. If she'd been wearing shoes she would have walked it easily, and saved herself the embarrassment of being forced to hug her unwanted rescuer, let alone be forced to travel with her face pressed against his muscular back.

When they reached the cottage, he insisted on dismounting and lifting her down.

'Thank you,' Allie said stiffly, trying not to overbalance. 'For—everything. I—I owe you a great deal.' She held out her hand. 'Goodbye, Dr de Brizat.'

His brows rose. 'Not Remy?'

'It's hardly appropriate,' she said, in a tone borrowed wholesale from Grace. 'After all, we're hardly likely to see each other after this.' She added pointedly, 'I don't intend to dice with death a second time.'

'Very wise, *ma belle*.' He took her hand and raised it swiftly to his lips, making her start at the casual intimacy. The pressure of his mouth and the graze of his unshaven chin against her fingers was an experience she could have well done without. 'Because tradition says that now I have saved your life it belongs to me, and I think you should live it to the full, and that I should help you to do so.'

He swung himself back into the saddle and grinned down at her. His teeth were very white against the darkness of his skin. 'And eventually,' he told her softly, 'you will call me Remy. I promise it. *Au revoir, ma chère* Alys.'

And, with a word to Roland, he cantered off, leaving Allie staring after him, aware of the sudden, uncomfortable flurry of her heartbeat.

As she went into the cottage Tante was just coming downstairs, trim and elegant in black tailored trousers and a white silk shirt, her silver hair confined at the nape of her neck with a black ribbon bow.

'My ears are playing tricks on me,' she complained. 'I thought I heard a horse outside…' She stopped, her eyes widening in alarm as she surveyed Allie. '*Mon Dieu, chérie*—what has happened to you?'

Allie sighed. 'I stupidly let myself get cut off by the tide,' she admitted. 'In a place called the Cauldron.'

'Alys.' Tante sat down limply on one of the kitchen

chairs. 'People have drowned there. You could have been one of them.'

Allie forced a smile. 'Except that your doctor's son came riding by, and gallantly carried me off across his saddle bow.' She stretched, wincing. 'I'm now a walking bruise.'

'It is no joking matter. You could have lost your life.'

'But I didn't. I'm simply minus a pair of shoes.'

Tante shuddered. 'You must never take such a chance again.'

'Believe me,' Alice said grimly, 'I don't intend to.'

'And it was Remy who saved you?' Tante made the sign of the cross. 'I shall go to see him, thank him for giving you back to me.' She brightened. 'Or, better, I shall invite him to dinner.'

Allie shifted restively from one bare foot to another. 'Is that strictly necessary? I did thank him myself, you know.' *After I'd taken a hell of a tongue-lashing.*

Tante pursed her lips. 'Madame Lastaine, who keeps house for the doctors at Trehel, is no cook,' she stated decisively. 'Remy will be glad of a good meal, *le pauvre.*'

'He seemed perfectly fit and healthy to me,' Allie said coolly.

Tante gave her a long look. 'Dear child, you seem—put out. Is it possible that you are blaming Remy in some way, because he did not let you drown?'

Allie bit her lip. 'Naturally, I'm grateful. But that doesn't mean I have to like him. Or that I have any wish for another encounter,' she added clearly, tilting her chin. 'And I hope his patients don't expect to receive any sympathy when they go to him.'

Tante's brows rose. She said mildly, 'I have never heard of any complaints about his attitude since he returned to Ignac. *Au contraire.* He is said to be skilful, and well-liked.'

Allie paused on her way to the stairs. 'He's not always worked here, then?' she asked, before she could stop herself.

'After he qualified he worked for a medical charity, firstly in Africa, then in South America. But it was always understood that he would one day fulfil the wishes of his father and grandfather and join the practice in Ignac.' Tante's smile was bland. 'I have always found him both charming and considerate. However, I shall not invite him here against your wishes, *chérie.*'

'Thank you.' Allie hesitated, her fingers beating a tattoo on the stair-rail. 'I just feel we're—better apart, that's all.'

*'D'accord.'* Tante's gaze shifted from her great-niece's flushed face to her restless hand. 'I notice that the sea took more than just your shoes, *ma mie*,' she remarked. 'It seems that your wedding ring, too, has gone.'

Allie's colour deepened. 'Not—entirely. It's upstairs. I—I simply decided not to wear it, that's all.'

'Ah,' Madelon Colville said meditatively. 'I am interested that you found that a simple decision.'

'I didn't mean it like that.' Allie took a deep breath.

'I took it off because I wanted to find the person I used to be—before my marriage. Somewhere along the way she seems to have vanished, but I really need to have her back.' She lifted her head. 'To be—Alys Colville again. Even if it's only for a little while.' She hesitated, sighing. 'But I suppose that's impossible. Everyone round here—all your neighbours—friends—will know I'm married. You must have mentioned it.'

'I told no one, *mon enfant*,' Tante said quietly. 'It was not news I ever wished to share. I have always believed that mistakes in one's family circle should be kept private. And I had known for some time—long before his tragic accident—that you did not love this man. Your letters made it clear.'

'But I hardly mentioned him.'

Tante's smile was kind. 'Exactly, *chérie*.' She paused. 'When I received the invitation to your wedding I wrote to your mother, begging her not to allow you to ruin your life. Saying that such a marriage would have profound difficulties, even if you adored each other.'

She shrugged wryly. 'Her reply was very angry. She said that I knew nothing about it. That you were devoted to your fiancé, that my interference was not needed, and it would be better for everyone if I stayed away.'

'She said you'd decided the journey would be too much for you.' Allie bit her lip. 'Oh—I should have known…'

'Well, that is all in the past now. It matters only that you are here now, *ma chère*. And if you wish to be Alys Colville again—then that is how it shall be.'

She became brisk. 'Now, go and change, and I will try to repair the damage the sea has done to those expensive clothes.'

Allie turned obediently, then paused. She said in a low voice, 'Am I crazy—to pretend like this?'

'Not crazy,' her great-aunt said slowly. 'But perhaps—not very wise.'

Allie's smile was swift and bleak. 'Then I'll just have to be very careful, too,' she said, and made her way to her room.

# CHAPTER THREE

THE sun had gone behind a cloud, and Allie got up from the bench, shivering a little.

She'd sat there long enough, she thought, tormenting herself with her memories. Now it was time to go back to the house and draft a letter to Tante, explaining why any return to Les Sables was impossible for her—now or in the future.

I can't do it, she told herself with anguish. Because, even now, the pain of that time is still too vivid and too raw.

She entered the house through a side door, and went straight upstairs. After Hugo's death, and in spite of Grace's protests, she'd moved out of the master suite she'd reluctantly shared with him into this smaller room at the back of the house. It wasn't as grand and formal as some of the others, and she liked its creamy-yellow walls, and the warm olive-green curtains and bedcover. Over the months it had become her refuge.

She sat down at the small writing table that she'd bought at an antique fair, and drew a sheet of paper towards her. She sat for a moment, tapping her pen against her teeth and staring out of the window in front of her, as she tried to come up with an excuse that her great-aunt would find even feasible, let alone acceptable.

Her room overlooked the vegetable garden, and the now-deserted stableyard. After the accident, Hugo's hunters had been sold, along with his polo ponies. Except, of course, for poor little Gimlet, who'd broken both forelegs in that terrible crashing fall in the final chukka, and had had to be put down on the field there and then.

'He was the lucky one,' Hugo had said with scalding bitterness when they'd told him. At that time he'd seemed to recognise the full extent of his injuries, Allie thought unhappily. It was later that he'd come to believe in his own self-will rather than the prognosis from the medical experts.

Sighing, she wrote the date. Well, it was a start, she told herself wryly, then paused as there was a swift tap on her door. It opened instantly to admit her mother-in-law.

'So there you are,' she commented. 'Mrs Windom has brought in the coffee. Are you coming down?'

'Later, perhaps. I'm replying to Tante Madelon's letter.'

'Ah.' Grace paused. 'Did she have anything particular to say?'

'She's not well,' Allie told her quietly. 'She'd like me to visit her—and take Tom with me.'

'No,' Lady Marchington said, swiftly and sharply.

'You can't possibly go to Brittany, and even if you did consider it you certainly couldn't take Tom. It's out of the question, Alice, and you know it.'

Allie found herself reeling back mentally under the onslaught.

Of choice, she wouldn't have mentioned Tante's letter, or its contents, precisely because she knew what the reaction would be. And because she had no intention of going.

Yet now she found herself bristling furiously, as a spirit of angry rebellion suddenly surged up inside her. This, she thought, is the last damned straw. I've had as much of her interference in my life as I can stand. I'm *not* living under a dictatorship, and it's time I made that clear.

She said coldly, 'I wouldn't be *allowed* to take my own child on holiday to visit a close relative? Is that really what you're saying?' She shook her head. 'I can't believe it.'

'Then you'd better suspend your disbelief.' Grace's expression was grim. 'I have no intention of permitting my grandson to be whisked out of the country—and to France, of all places.'

'Why not? Was one of the Marchington ancestors killed at Agincourt?' Allie tried to speak lightly, in spite of the anger building inside her.

'Don't be flippant,' Grace snapped. 'What I'm saying is that our lives are not going to be turned upside down at the behest of one arrogant old woman. I simply won't permit it.'

'Please don't speak about Tante like that,' Allie said icily. 'The invitation came to me, and I'll deal with it as I see fit.' She paused, steadying her breathing. 'I'm not a child. I'm twenty-two years old, and I don't need your permission, or anyone else's for that matter, to stay in Brittany with the woman who practically brought up my father.'

She met Lady Marchington's furious gaze in open challenge. 'Anyway, why shouldn't I go? Give me one good reason.' *If you dare...*

Spots of colour burned in the older woman's face. 'Tom's far too young for a journey of that nature.'

'A night on a ferry and a couple of hours by car?' Allie's tone was derisive. 'Babies far younger make similar trips every day.'

'But Tom isn't just any child. He's the Marchington heir. You have your position to consider. And his.'

Allie's gaze remained stony. 'And is that your only objection? Because Tom isn't just a Marchington. He has Colville and Vaillac blood too. And it's entirely natural that Tante should want to see him, especially as she's in bad health. After all, he's the last of her line, too.'

Grace's mouth hardened. 'Breton peasant stock. Hardly anything to boast about.'

'They're brave, and strong, with good, loving hearts,' Allie returned icily. 'That would be enough for most people.'

'Now you're just being difficult.'

'Under the circumstances,' Allie said, 'that is almost amusing. Only I don't feel like laughing.'

'Alice—for heaven's sake. There was enough talk last time when you simply—disappeared, for weeks on end, leaving poor Hugo to cope alone.'

'Hardly alone. He had you, his nanny, a full-time nurse, and all the staff to look after him. I was pretty much surplus to requirements—except in one respect, of course.'

She paused. 'And I came back. As I always intended. Was there more talk then? Or did I redeem myself because at last I was doing my duty by my brave, disabled husband, and giving him the child he'd been demanding with such monotonous regularity?'

There was another taut silence.

'Sometimes,' Grace said, 'you sound so hard, Alice.'

'Do I?' Allie's smile didn't reach her eyes. 'I wonder why?'

'And I'm hurt that you should be making this kind of decision without consulting me.'

You, thought Allie, wouldn't be hurt even if I hammered a stake through your heart.

'As soon as that letter arrived I knew exactly what that woman would want,' Grace added angrily.

'Oh, come on,' Allie defended. 'You talk as if Tante's always demanding attention, and that's simply not true.'

'Oh, she's more subtle than that,' her mother-in-law said derisively. 'Your mother warned me, of course, that she was a born manipulator.'

Well, the pair of you should know, Allie countered silently.

'Well, let's agree to disagree over that too, shall we?' she suggested quietly.

'And French houses don't have proper damp-proof courses.' Grace tried a new tack. 'Tom might catch a chill.'

Alice leaned back in her chair. 'He doesn't stay still for long enough. And I don't want him wrapped in cotton wool all the time. He's a little boy, for heaven's sake.'

'Yes, he is, and I'm not sure you realise just how important he is to the future of the Marchingtons.'

'On the contrary. I've had it drummed into me that he *is* the future of the Marchingtons, God help him.' Alice said shortly. 'Before, during and after he was born, God help *me*.'

There was a silence. Then Lady Marchington said, 'Alice, listen—please.' She looked older suddenly, and weary. Almost scared. 'You can't possibly go back to that place. It would be madness.'

There were two heartbeats of silence as Allie looked back at her. Her voice was even. 'In what way—madness?'

Her mother-in-law put up a hand to smooth her already immaculate hair. 'Well—perhaps madness is a slight exaggeration. All the same, you must see why you shouldn't go back there. And I'm sure your mother would agree with me.'

'I don't doubt it,' Allie returned quietly. 'But it makes no difference to my decision.'

Lady Marchington took a deep breath. 'If Madelon

genuinely wishes to see Tom, perhaps—arrangements could be made for her to come to England.'

'Except that it isn't right to uproot someone of her age,' Alice said quietly. 'Particularly when she's unwell, and I'm young and healthy and can make the trip perfectly easily.'

*What am I saying? Why am I making all these arguments for a case I'd already decided to lose? Because it's too late to say so. Because, by this totally unwanted and unwarranted intervention, Grace has backed me into a corner, and if I'm ever to establish any independence for myself I cannot give way over this issue. And, as a result, I now have to go back to Les Sables d'Ignac, even though it's the last thing I want in this world.*

*I have to. There's no choice now. It's make or break time…*

*Oh, God, why couldn't she have kept quiet? Given me the chance to find some kind of valid excuse for staying away. For escaping this nightmare?*

'Plymouth to Roscoff overnight,' she added with a shrug, forcing herself to sound casual. 'Then a leisurely drive down to Les Sables. Tom will love it.'

'You can't take Tom,' Grace said harshly. 'If you insist on going, it must be alone.'

'You mean that after deserting my husband on the last visit, I should desert my son this time?' Allie asked ironically. 'Imagine the gossip that would cause. And I don't choose to feature as a neglectful mother. Besides,' she added squarely. 'It would give me the

chance to really *be* with Tom for once. To spend some
real quality time with him on my own, so that we can
get to know each other properly.'

'On your own? But you'll have to take Nanny.'

When hell freezes over…

Aloud, 'Thank you,' she said politely. 'But I
wouldn't dream of it. I'm perfectly capable of driving
my own car, and caring for Tom like any other mother.
In fact, I'll love it. Besides,' she added practically,
'Tante has no room for another guest at the cottage,
and it's the holiday season over there.'

I want my life back, and I want my child back too,
she thought. And if this is the only way, then I'll take it.

Grace clearly realised she had lost the advantage,
and her mouth was a slit. But her voice was composed
again. 'I see. So, when are you thinking of going?'

'I thought—as soon as I can get a ferry booking.'
Allie looked back at her calmly, just as if her stomach
wasn't tying itself into knots at the prospect. She
added, 'I think I'll pass on the coffee. Tante will be
waiting for my reply.'

Grace nodded. 'Then clearly there's nothing more to
be said.' She gave a small wintry nod, and left the room.

The ferry was crowded, and it seemed to take an age
before her deck was cleared and Allie was able to
drive down the ramp into the busy port of Roscoff.

It was a clear, bright morning, but the crossing had
been a choppy one. Tom had not liked the motion of
the ship, and had proclaimed as much all night long.

He'd not been sick, just angry and frightened—and probably missing Nanny's confident, capable handling, Allie acknowledged exhaustedly. And for the first time she wondered if Grace and her mother had been right. She was too inexperienced, and he was too young for such a trip.

But, as she'd waited restlessly to be called to her car, she'd seen umpteen other babies, much younger than hers, who seemed perfectly relaxed and cheerful about the whole experience.

It's all my own fault, she told herself, for not insisting on looking after him myself from Day One, and to hell with postnatal depression. Other women manage, and I could have done, too. Well, from now on things are going to change. Permanently.

She couldn't pretend it would be easy. Nanny had greeted the news of the trip in ominous silence, and the days leading up to departure had been cloaked in an atmosphere that could only have been cut by a chainsaw.

But, when Allie had taken no notice, she'd been forced to accept the situation.

It might not be a very worthy triumph, thought Allie, but for someone who'd been consistently ignored since Tom was born, and made to feel incompetent and ungrateful when she protested, it was eminently satisfying.

She got well free of Roscoff and its environs, then stopped at a *tabac* in a convenient village, ordering a *café au lait* and a croissant, while Tom had milk, and made himself agreeably messy with a *pain au chocolat*.

She gave him a perfunctory wipe down to remove the worst of the crumbs, then strapped him back into his safety seat with his favourite blue rabbit. Before they'd gone half a mile, the combination of the previous restless night and warm food caught up with him, and he fell peacefully and soundly asleep, leaving Allie to concentrate on her driving.

Last time she'd come this way, she'd pushed the car swiftly, almost recklessly, aware of little but her own wretchedness, but now she had precious cargo on board, and her control was absolute. She slotted some cool jazz into the CD player, and headed steadily south towards Ignac, knowing that she would easily reach Tante's house by lunchtime.

Tom slept for an hour and a half, and then woke, grizzling. Allie parked on the wide verge at the side of the road, changed him quickly, gave him a drink, then let him play on the rug she'd spread on the grass. Propped on an elbow, she watched him, smiling, as he carefully dismembered a large leaf.

He turned his head and saw her, according her the sudden vivid grin that lit up his face, before stumping energetically in her direction, grabbing her shoulder to steady himself.

'Who's my wonderful, clever boy?' she praised, hugging him. And who certainly *isn't* going to be bow-legged through walking too soon? she added silently, recalling a recent bone of contention at home.

They stayed for another sunlit half-hour before Allie decided they should be on their way again. Tom made a token protest as he was strapped into his baby seat, but she soon tickled him into good humour again, nuzzling her face into his neck so that he laughed and grabbed at her hair.

An hour and a half later, Ignac began appearing on the signposts. She saw the name with a sense of relief, because it had been a long time since she'd undertaken so long a drive. Although so far it had been an easy, even enjoyable journey, with only moderate traffic to contend with in places.

The joys of midweek travel, she thought. Most of the holidaymakers arrived at the weekend, and are now relaxing at their hotels and *gîtes*, leaving the roads open for me, bless them.

*'Courage, mon brave,'* she told Tom, who was beginning to be restive again. 'We're nearly there.'

Mentally, however, she was already bracing herself, unsure of what she might find when she reached Les Sables.

Tante disliked the telephone, regarding it as something to be used only in the direst emergencies, and the letter expressing her delight at Allie's visit, and confirming the suggested arrangements, had been in the same wavering hand as before.

Not for the first time, Allie wished there was someone she could confide in about her worries. Someone who also cared about Tante.

Once there was, she thought—and stopped right there, her lips tightening. She could not let herself remember that—even though every landmark—every direction sign in the last hour—had been battering at her memory with their own poignant reminders.

But what else could she have expected? she asked herself with a sigh. Those few brief weeks with Remy had given her the only real happiness she'd ever known. How could she even pretend she'd forgotten?

Tante had warned she would find Ignac much changed, but apart from the new villas, all white and terracotta in the sunlight, which had sprung up like mushrooms on the outskirts, the little town seemed much the same.

Its church was ordinary, and Ignac didn't possess one of the elaborately carved calvaries which were among the great sights of the region, but its busy fishing harbour bestowed a quiet charm of its own.

The narrow streets were already crammed, with parked cars on both sides, and as she negotiated them with care she realised that the town square ahead was a mass of striped awnings.

'Of course,' she said aloud. 'It's market day. I certainly forgot about that.'

The market was drawing to its close, the stalls being swiftly dismantled, rails of clothing and boxes of household goods being put back in vans, although last-minute shoppers still lingered at the food stalls, hoping for bargains.

But we, she thought, always came early to buy…

She forced her attention back to the road ahead, braking gently as an old lady stumped out on to the pedestrian crossing just ahead, waving her stick to signify her right to priority. She was accompanied, apprehensively, by a younger couple, and as she reached the middle of the crossing she stopped suddenly, and turned to upbraid them about something, using her stick for emphasis. The other woman looked at Allie, shrugging in obvious embarrassment, as all efforts to get the senior member of the party moving again ended in stalemate.

She wants to have her say, and she wants it now, Allie thought, reluctantly amused. And, until it's over, we're going nowhere.

People were pausing to watch, and smile, as if this was a familiar occurrence.

He seemed to come from nowhere, but there he was, joining the trio on the crossing, a tall, lean figure, dark and deeply tanned, casual in cream jeans and an open-necked blue shirt. He was carrying two long loaves of bread, and a plastic bag that Allie knew would contain oysters. He transferred it to his other hand, before he bent, speaking softly to the old lady, while his fingers cupped her elbow leading her, gently but firmly, to the opposite pavement.

For a moment it looked as if she might resist, then the wrinkled face broke into an unwilling grin and he laughed too, lifting her hand to his lips with swift grace. Then, with a quick word and a shrug to her grateful companions, he was gone again, vanishing between the remaining market stalls as quickly as he'd arrived.

Allie sat and watched him go, her hands gripping the

wheel as if they'd been glued there. She thought numbly, But it *can't* be him. It can't be Remy because Tante said—she promised—that I'd have nothing to fear.

*Nothing to fear…*

An impatient hooting from the vehicles behind brought her back to the here and now, and she realised, embarrassment flooding her face with colour, that the total shock of seeing him had made her stall the engine. She restarted carefully, and set off, waving an apologetic hand to the other drivers.

She threaded her way out of town and on to the narrow road which led to Les Sables, before yanking the wheel over and bringing the car to an abrupt halt. She sat for a moment, her whole body shaking, then flung open the car door and stumbled out, kneeling on the short, scrubby grass while she threw up.

As she straightened, her head swimming, her throat and stomach aching, she heard Tom's frightened wail from the car, and dragged herself to her feet in instant contrition.

'It's all right, darling, Mummy's here.' She found a packet of wipes in the glove compartment and hastily cleaned her face and hands, before releasing Tom from his harness and lifting him into her arms. She sat down on a flat boulder a few feet away from the car, and held him close against her, patting him and murmuring soothingly while she waited for her heartbeat to settle. And she tried desperately to make sense of what had just happened. But failed.

*There is nothing that should keep you away…*

The words were indelibly printed on her brain. Unforgettable.

The wording of Tante's letter had suggested—had seemed to promise—that Remy was still far off in South America. So how could he possibly be there in Ignac, charming tough old ladies into compliance, buying food from the market, clearly as much at home as if he'd never been away?

*She should have told me the truth,* she thought passionately. *Should have warned me that he was here. Except that if she had nothing would have dragged me here, and she knew it.*

*Perhaps,* she thought, *Tante doesn't know he's come back. Maybe it's a temporary thing—some kind of furlough—and she hasn't heard.*

But she discounted that almost at once. Her aunt's house might be secluded, but it wasn't in limbo. Every piece of gossip, every item of local news, found its way to her sooner or later.

Besides, Remy's father, Philippe de Brizat, was Tante's doctor—and his father before him, for all she knew.

Of course the news of Remy's return would have been shared with her.

Anguish stabbed at her. It seemed unbelievable that her beloved and trusted great-aunt should have deliberately set out to deceive her like this. Unless she knew that the first time she did so would also be the last.

*She must,* Allie thought sombrely, *be really desper-*

ate to see me again—to see Tom—even to contemplate such a thing.

Her immediate instinct was to turn the car and drive back to Roscoff. Get the first possible return sailing. But, apart from all the other considerations, that would mean returning to the Hall with her tail between her legs, losing any advantage she'd gained in her belated bid for independence.

I could still visit Tante, she thought, but make it a brief visit—not stay for the ten days as planned. That should be safe enough.

After all, France is a big country, and Brittany's not its only region. Plus, it's still early enough in the year for there to be hotel vacancies. I could take Tom exploring the Auvergne, or the Dordogne. Even go as far as the Côte d'Azur.

Anywhere, she resolved, as long as it was far—far away from Remy de Brizat. Because Tante was so terribly wrong, and she had *everything* to fear from encountering him again.

Her arms closed more tightly around Tom, who wriggled in protest, demanding to be set down.

She held his hands, steering him back to the car as he paced unsteadily along, face set in fierce determination.

'I know the feeling,' she told him as she lifted him back into his seat for the short drive to Les Sables. 'And from now on, my love, it's you and me against the world.'

The house stood alone, grey and solid against the slender clustering pine trees behind it. Allie eased the car along the track, remembering her father's concern that Tante should have chosen such an isolated spot.

'It wouldn't do for me,' he'd said, shaking his head. 'The silence would drive me crazy.'

Tante had laughed gently. 'But there is no silence, *mon cher*. I live between the wind singing in the trees and the sound of the sea. It is more than enough.'

The front door was open, Allie saw, and a woman's small, upright figure had emerged, and was standing, shading her eyes against the sun, watching the car approach.

It's Tante Madelon, Allie realised with astonishment. But if she's been ill, surely she should be in bed, or at least resting on the sofa.

She brought the car to a halt on the gravelled area in front of the house and paused for a moment, taking a deep breath. She'd already decided on her strategy. No reproaches or recriminations. Instead, she too would practise a deception—she would pretend that she'd simply driven through Ignac and seen no one. As far as she was concerned, Remy de Brizat was still on the other side of the world.

And if Tante mentioned his being back in Ignac, she would produce a look of faint surprise, maybe even risk a polite question about his life in Brazil. Or had he, in fact, moved on from there?

She'd tried so hard not to think about that. Not to wonder where he was and what he was doing.

And now it seemed as if all her desperate efforts to blank him out of her mind had been in vain.

Ah, well, she thought bleakly, as she marshalled her defences. Just as long as it doesn't show.

And she opened the car door and got out, smiling resolutely.

Madelon Colville had never been a large woman, but now she seemed to have shrunk even more. In Allie's embrace, she felt as insubstantial as a captured bird. But her eyes were still bright, shining with love and pleasure, and her voice was husky with emotion as she murmured words of welcome.

'Dearest child, you cannot know what this means to me.' She looked towards the car with unconcealed eagerness. 'Now, where is your little son?'

Finding himself on show, Tom decided to be shy, and buried his face in his mother's neck. But Tante was unfazed by the reaction.

'It is all too new and strange for him,' she declared. 'But soon we will be friends—won't we, *chéri*?' She took Allie's hand. 'Now, come in, and meet Madame Drouac, who looks after me. She is a widow, like myself, and so good to me. However, she speaks no English, and you will not understand her *patois*, so I shall translate for you both.'

Madame Drouac, who was standing at the range, stirring a pan of something that smelt deliciously savoury, was a tall, angular woman with a calm face and kind, shrewd eyes. As she shook hands, Allie was aware of being subjected to a searching look, followed by a low-voiced exchange with her great-aunt.

But Allie did not need a translation. She remembers

me from the last time I was here, she told herself without pleasure. Recalls who I was with, too.

'Amelie thinks you have become thin, *ma mie*.' Madelon spoke lightly. 'She says we must fill you with good food. Also *le petit*.'

She indicated an old-fashioned wooden highchair, polished to within an inch of its life, which was standing at the table. 'She has loaned us this for Thomas. Also the cot, where her own son slept. He has married a girl from Rennes,' she added with a shrug. 'And she does not need them for her baby. She wants everything that is new. So Amelie is pleased that her things will be used once more.'

She paused. 'I have told her that you are a widow, Alys, but also that your marriage only occurred after you left here and returned to England.' Her gaze was steady. 'You understand?'

'Yes,' Allie said woodenly. 'Yes, of course.'

Lunch was a thick vegetable soup, served with chunks of bread, and there was cheese to follow.

Tom made a spirited attack on his soup, using his spoon like a stabbing spear. He was assisted in his efforts by Madame Drouac, who talked softly to him in Breton, and occasionally clucked at him like a hen, which provoked a joyous toothy grin. Shyness, it seemed, was a thing of the past, Allie saw with relief.

'He usually has a nap in the afternoon,' she mentioned as they drank their coffee.

'Very wise,' said Tante. 'I do the same.' She gave

Allie a long look. 'And perhaps you should rest also, *ma mie*. You are pale, and your eyes are tired.'

'Well, I have had more peaceful nights,' Allie admitted ruefully. She hesitated. 'Would it be all right if I took a shower first? I feel as if I've been wearing these clothes for ever.'

Tante covered her hand with her own. 'You must do exactly as you wish, *chérie*. This is your other home. You know that.'

It's probably my only real home, Allie thought, as she carried Tom upstairs. The room had been rearranged, with its wide bed pushed under the window in order to accommodate the cot—a palatial, beautifully carved affair. For a moment, Allie felt almost sorry for the daughter-in-law from Rennes who couldn't recognise a family heirloom when she saw it. But her loss was Tom's gain, and he was asleep even before Allie had finished unpacking.

She undressed slowly, and put on her thin, white silk dressing gown before making her way to the bathroom, which boasted a separate shower cabinet as well as a large tub. 'It may be a cottage, but I insist on my comforts,' Madelon Colville had declared, when the old-fashioned fittings had been torn out and replaced.

And maybe I like mine too, Allie thought wryly, as she set out the array of exquisitely scented toiletries she'd brought with her.

She stepped into the shower and turned on the spray, letting the water cascade luxuriously over her hair and body.

The soup had been just what she needed, and, although she was still on edge, she was no longer shaking inside. Madame Drouac was clearly a good cook, and Allie found she was looking forward to the casserole of lamb that had been promised for the evening meal.

'Amelie is a jewel,' Tante had said quietly downstairs. 'I only wish she was not considered a necessity. But the doctor insisted I should have help.'

*The doctor…* But which one did Madelon Colville mean? After all, there were three generations of de Brizats living at the big stone house at Trehel. It could hardly be the grandfather, Georges, who had retired under protest a few years before and must now be nearing his eighties, so it had to be Philippe still—or his only son, Allie thought, biting her lip savagely. And that was something she couldn't ask.

She wished that Madame Drouac spoke even a little English, so that, among other things, she could establish exactly what was wrong with her great-aunt. Because, when she'd tried a little tactful probing, Tante had merely waved a languid hand and said that she had good days and bad ones.

'But today is nothing but good, because you are here,' she'd added.

On the other hand, Allie thought wryly, the language barrier between the housekeeper and herself meant she didn't have to answer any awkward questions about her previous stay.

She towelled herself dry, and slipped on her robe

again. Back in the bedroom, she combed her damp hair into place, reluctant to use her dryer in case she disturbed Tom.

In spite of her weariness, she knew she would not sleep. She was too tense, and her brain was buzzing. She knew that for her own peace of mind she should have stayed away. That she should not have let herself be provoked into accepting such a dangerous invitation. But could she really regret what she'd done, when Tante was so clearly overjoyed to see her?

And, anyway, it was far too late for repining.

The box was unlocked at last, and all her personal demons had come swarming into the open. And somehow they had to be faced. Whatever the personal pain they might bring in their wake.

# CHAPTER FOUR

SHE knelt on the bed, resting her arms on the window ledge, staring down at the bay where it had all begun.

*Not very wise…*

That was what Madelon had told her in warning, she thought, and it was probably the understatement of the decade. But how could I know where it would lead? After all, I only wanted some time to myself—to think, and make some decisions. And I didn't wish to be cross-examined, however kindly, over where my husband was, or why he wasn't with me.

I just—needed some peace.

I never meant there to be more to it than that. And I certainly never intended to deceive anyone, or cause any hurt.

Plus, I didn't lie. I just didn't tell the whole truth and nothing but the truth.

But then no one actually asked me to do so—or not until it was so much too late.

She stopped herself right there. She could play with words and motives for ever, but nothing could actually justify what she'd done. She'd desperately needed to be honest, and instead she'd crashed in flames. And she could blame nothing and no one but herself.

Yet here she was, two years on, knowing that she could not afford to be completely frank. That there were still things that could not be said.

A widow with a child, she thought. That was all anyone needed to know.

And although Remy might be back in Ignac, that did not necessarily imply they would meet.

On the contrary, she told herself with resolution, she would go out of her way to ensure they didn't.

I dare not risk it, she thought. For all kinds of reasons…

Sighing, she swung herself off the bed, pulling on shorts, a vest top and sandals, then went over to the cot. Tom was still fast asleep, chubby arms tossed wide, and her heart lurched as she looked down at him.

When Tante was gone, he would be all she had left to love. But he made all the agony of the past seem somehow worthwhile. She smoothed the damp, dark curls with a gentle finger, but he did not stir, so she tiptoed from the room and went slowly downstairs. The living room was empty, so presumably Madame Drouac had returned to her own abode for the afternoon, and the sun was streaming in through the open door at the rear.

Allie, drawing a deep, unsteady breath, walked out into the walled garden beyond.

The wind had dropped, and there were just a few faint streaks of high cloud, motionless against the baking blue of the sky.

She sat down on the grass, her back against the solitary ancient apple tree, and stared upwards, shading her eyes with her hand. So many days like this, she thought, breathing in the scent of earth and sun-warmed grass. So many memories jarring her mind again. Splintering her inner calm. Waiting inexorably to be dealt with.

Closing her eyes, Allie, slowly and reluctantly, allowed herself to surrender to the pull of the past.

In the days following her ruthless and spectacular rescue by Remy de Brizat, she'd made a conscious decision to keep well away from the beach, even though Tante had supplied her with a tide table and told her to learn it by heart.

But, in her heart, Allie knew that the rise and fall of the sea wasn't the principal danger to be encountered.

The weather had turned intensely hot, giving her a good excuse to remain quietly in the seclusion of the garden, sunbathing and reading, as she felt her inner tensions begin to slip gently away. Or most of them, anyway.

One morning, over breakfast, Tante had mentioned that she was driving to Quimper later, to visit her accountant. 'Some papers to do with tax, *chérie*, and so boring. But you are welcome to come with me, if you wish.'

Allie had decided she did not wish. She'd waved goodbye to Madelon, then taken her rug and cushion into the garden and stretched out face downward, unclipping her bikini top with a languid hand as she did so. But the hum of insects, the whisper of the leaves, and the distant murmur of the sea had failed for once to have their usual soporific effect. She'd felt oddly restless, and even the thriller she'd been reading had palled, its plot descending, she had decided, into sheer absurdity.

She'd tossed it aside, pillowed her head on her arms, and closed her eyes, making a deliberate effort to relax her whole body, commencing with her toes, then working slowly upward. Any moment now, she'd promised herself, she would feel completely calm.

'*Bonjour*, Alys.'

For a shocked second, she thought she'd dozed off and was actually dreaming, but one startled sideways glance revealed battered espadrilles and, rising out of them, a pair of long, tanned and totally masculine legs.

'You?' She almost sat up, remembering just in time her loosened top. 'What are you doing here?'

'I wished to make sure that the events of the other morning had left no lasting trauma.' He grinned down at her, totally at his ease, casual in shorts and a cotton shirt unbuttoned almost to the waist.

'And is this how you normally make house calls?' It was difficult, she found, to glare at someone effectively when you were forced to lie prone, and all they could see was your profile. 'Just—march in without knocking or asking permission?' *And half-dressed?*

'No,' he said. 'But this is not a professional visit, you understand. Also, I met with Madame Colville on the road, and she gave me leave to visit you.'

He looked her over with undisguised appreciation, his eyes lingering, she realised furiously, on the narrow band of jade fabric that scarcely masked the swell of her buttocks.

'The sun is fierce today,' he said softly. 'And you should not risk burning such lovely skin.' He knelt down beside her, reaching for the bottle of sun lotion. He tipped some into the palm of his hand and began to apply it to her shoulders, in smooth, delicate strokes.

For a moment she was rendered mute with shock, then hurriedly pulled herself together.

'Thank you,' she said through gritted teeth. 'But I'm quite capable of doing that for myself.'

'*Vraiment?*' His brows lifted in polite enquiry, but he made no attempt to bring his unwanted ministrations to an end. 'You are, perhaps, a *contorsionniste*? No? Then be still, and allow me to do this for you.'

His light, assured touch on her skin sent alarm signals quivering along her nerve-endings.

I don't want this, she thought almost frantically. I—really do not...

She would have given anything to be able to sit up and snatch the damned bottle from his hand, but she was anchored to the rug. If only—*only*—she hadn't unfastened her top. And the fact that he must have seen hundreds of women with bare breasts in his career made not an atom of difference.

Because Remy de Brizat was not her doctor, and, for all his comments about trauma, she was not his patient and never would be.

He took all the time in the world, his hands lingering, while Allie, raging with the knowledge of her own temporary helplessness, lay with her eyes shut and her bottom lip caught between her teeth as she fought a losing battle over the slow, inevitable awakening of her senses.

This can't be happening to me, she thought. It just can't.

One of the reasons I ran away was because I didn't want to be touched—because I couldn't bear it any longer.

And this man—this stranger—has no right to make me feel like this—as if my skin was made of silk, and my bones were dissolving. He has no right at all.

At last he paused, running a light finger along the rim of her bikini briefs but venturing no further, and she released her held breath, thinking that her ordeal was over.

Only to find herself stifling a startled whimper when he began to anoint the backs of her thighs, moving gently down to reach the sensitive area in the bend of her knees.

'*Alors.*' With sudden briskness, he recapped the bottle and put it down beside her. 'The rest I am sure you can manage for yourself.'

'Thank you,' she said with icy politeness. 'But I think I've had enough sun for one day.'

'Perhaps you are wise,' he said, faint amusement in his voice. 'Why take more risks with such a charming body?'

Her throat tightened. 'Thank you for your concern,' she said. 'But I can look after myself.'

She fumbled for the edges of her bra top and tried to bring them together across her slippery skin, with fingers made clumsy through haste.

'Of course—as you prove so constantly, *ma belle.*' She could hear him smiling, damn him. *'Permettez-moi.'* He took the strips of material from her, and deftly hooked them into place.

*Too bloody deftly altogether…*

She sat up, pushing her hair back from her flushed face with a defensive hand. 'Does that fulfil your quota of good deeds for the day?' she asked stiffly. 'Or do you have other visits to make? Because I wouldn't wish to delay you on your errands of mercy.'

He studied her for a moment. 'Why do you speak to me as if I were your enemy, Alys?'

Her colour deepened. 'I—don't,' she denied shortly.

'No?' His mouth twisted wryly. 'Then I hope we do not meet when you wish to be hostile.'

She took a swift breath. 'I would actually prefer it, *monsieur*, if we didn't meet at all after this.' She lifted her chin. 'You got me out of a nasty situation the other day, and I shall always be grateful for that. But now I would really like to be left in peace to—to enjoy my vacation without any further intervention from you. I'm sure you understand.'

'I think I begin to,' Remy de Brizat said slowly. 'Tell me, Alys, do all men make you so nervous, or is it just myself?'

She gasped. 'I'm not the slightest bit nervous—of you, or anyone.'

'Then prove it,' he said, 'together with this gratitude you say you feel, and have lunch with me tomorrow.'

'Lunch?' she echoed in disbelief. 'But why should I do any such thing?'

He shrugged. 'I have already given you two good reasons,' he said. 'Besides, everyone needs to eat, and midday is considered a convenient time by most people.' The blue eyes considered her again, more thoroughly. 'And you are a little underweight, you know.'

She lifted her chin. 'Is that in your medical opinion, or for your personal taste?' she queried coldly.

He grinned at her. 'I think—both.'

Well, she'd asked for that, but it didn't improve her temper or weaken her resolve to keep him at bay.

He had a proud face, she thought, stealing a lightning glance at him from under her lashes. There was even a hint of arrogance in the high cheekbones and the cool lines of his mouth.

This was a man who was almost certainly unused to rejection, and equally unlikely to take it well.

I don't suppose, Allie mused, he's ever been stood up in his life. And—who knows?—it might teach him a much-needed lesson. And, more importantly, it will demonstrate that I'm not available. Let's hope he takes the hint.

She shrugged a bare shoulder, half smiling, as if resigned to her fate.

'Very well, then. Lunch it is. As you say, we all need to eat.' She paused. 'What do you propose?'

There was a brief silence, then he said slowly,

'There is a good restaurant on the road towards Benodet—Chez Lucette. You think you can find it?'

'Of course.'

'*Bon.* Then, shall we say—twelve-thirty?'

'Perfect.' Allie looked down demurely. 'I—look forward to it, *monsieur.*'

His brows lifted. 'Still not Remy?'

'After lunch,' she said, and smiled. 'Perhaps.'

He said softly, 'I shall live in hope. *A bientôt.*' And went.

Left alone, Allie realised she was as breathless as if she'd been running in some marathon. It was a reaction she was not accustomed to, and it scared her.

All I had to do, she thought, swallowing, was tell him, *'I'm married.'* And he would never have troubled me again. It was that simple. So why didn't I say it? Why let him go on thinking I'm single? Available?

Oh, stop beating yourself up, she adjured herself impatiently. As long as you brush him off, why worry about the method? And after tomorrow he certainly won't be coming round again.

She would change her brand of sun oil, too, she decided broodingly. Find an alternative with a different scent—one that wouldn't remind her of the play of his hands as he massaged it into her warm skin each time she smelt it.

She said aloud, 'Whatever it takes, I *will* be left in peace. And to hell with Remy de Brizat.'

* * *

'Are you quite well, *chérie*?' Tante studied her anxiously. 'You seem tense—restless—this morning.'

'I'm fine,' Allie assured her, wandering out into the garden to sneak a look at her watch. Twenty-five past twelve, she thought. Excellent. He should be at Chez Lucette by now, and ordering his aperitif. Probably looking at his watch too, gauging my arrival.

I wonder how long he'll wait before it dawns on him that he's struck out for once? That I've not simply been delayed, but that I shan't be joining him at all?

And what will he do then? Eat alone at his table for two? Or pretend he has an urgent case to go to before the egg hardens on his face?

Whatever—it serves him right, she told herself defensively, although she was totally unable to rationalise this conviction.

And she was sure there were plenty of ladies in the locality who would be happy to help soothe his bruised ego, she added, ramming her clenched hands into the pockets of her skirt.

'Alys?' Tante was calling from the back door, surprise in her voice. 'Alys, you have a visitor.'

She swung round just in time to see Remy de Brizat walk out into the garden. He was dressed much as he had been the day before, with emphasis on the casual, his sunglasses pushed up on his forehead.

For a moment, Allie could only gape at him. When she spoke, her voice was husky with shock. 'What are you doing here? I—I don't understand…'

His smile was sardonic. 'I decided against the restaurant after all, *ma belle*. It occurred to me that you would have difficulties in getting there. So I put food and wine in the car so that we can picnic instead.' He added solicitously, 'I hope you are not too disappointed?'

'No,' she said. 'That's not the word I'd have chosen.' She swallowed. 'How did you know that I wouldn't meet you?'

He shrugged. 'One minute you were spitting at me like a little cat. The next you were—honey. It was too much of a *volte face* to be entirely credible.'

'And, of course, you wouldn't just take the hint and stay away?'

'I considered it.'

'Then why are you here?'

'Because you intrigue me, Alys. Enough, certainly, to risk another rebuff.' He added softly, 'Also, I still wish to hear you call me Remy.'

He held out his hand. 'It's only lunch, *ma mie*. Shall we go?'

Is it? she thought, feeling the rapid thud of her heart. Is that really all it is?

Tell him, counselled the warning voice in her head. Tell him the truth now. Say that you misled him the other day because you were upset and didn't know what you were saying. That it wouldn't be appropriate for you to see each other again because you have a husband in England.

Then it will be over, and you won't have to worry any more. You want peace of mind? Then take it. Because this could be your last chance.

And she found herself looking down at herself—at the thin blouse, the straight white skirt and the strappy sandals. Heard herself saying, 'I—I'd better change. I'm not really dressed for a picnic.'

'You look enchanting,' he said. 'But—just as you wish.'

Her glance was scornful. 'Now, we both know that isn't true.'

Inside the house, Tante looked at her, her forehead puckered in concern. 'My dear child, are you sure you know what you're doing?'

'Yes,' Allie said, and paused to kiss her cheek. 'It's fine, really,' she whispered. 'We're just going to have lunch—one meal together. And that's all.'

Then I'll tell him I'm married, she thought as she ran upstairs. And it will finally be finished.

Madness, Allie thought, returning bleakly to the here and now as tears burned in the back of her eyes and choked her throat. Sweet, compelling, uncontrollable madness. That was what it had been—how it had been.

One man—*the man*—was all it had taken to breach the firewall around her. Just the touch of his hand had altered all her perceptions of herself, destroying once and for all the myth of her invulnerable reserve.

How could she have known that she'd simply been waiting—waiting for him? Remy…

His name was a scream in her heart.

She drew her knees up to her chin, bent her head, and allowed herself to cry. The house was asleep, so thankfully there was no one to hear her agonised keening or the sobs that threatened to rip her apart.

For two years she'd had to suppress her emotions and rebuild her defences. Never allowing herself to reveal even for a moment the inner pain that was threatening to destroy her.

Now, at last, the dam had burst, and she yielded to the torrent of grief and guilt it had released, rocking backwards and forwards, her arms wrapped round her knees. Until, eventually, she could cry no more.

Then, when the shaking had stopped, she got slowly to her feet, brushing fronds of dried grass from her clothing, and went into the house.

She washed her face thoroughly, removing all traces of the recent storm, then carefully applied drops to her eyes, before returning to her room. Tom had not stirred, and she stretched herself on the bed, waiting with quiet patience for him to wake up, and for the rest of her life to begin.

She must have dozed, because she suddenly became aware, with a start, that he was standing, vigorously rattling the bars of his cot. As she swung herself off the bed and went to him, he gave his swift, entrancing grin, and held out his arms.

She picked him up, rubbing noses with him. 'And hi there to you too. Want to play outside?'

Tante was there ahead of them this time, sitting placidly under a green and white striped parasol, her hands busy with her favourite embroidery, a jug of home-made lemonade on the wooden table at her elbow.

She looked up, smiling. 'Did you rest well, *chérie*?'

'It was good not to be moving,' Allie evaded. She put Tom down on the blanket that had already been spread on the grass in anticipation, rolling his coloured ball across the grass for him to chase before sitting down and accepting the glass of lemonade that Tante poured for her.

And now it was high time to face a few issues. And with honesty, this time around, if that was possible.

'I came across a little drama in Ignac today,' she remarked, trying to sound casual. 'A fierce old lady having some family battle in the middle of the road, and refusing to give way.'

Tante chose another length of silk from the box beside her. 'That would be Madame Teglas,' she said composedly. '*Pauvre femme*, she hates her unfortunate daughter-in-law, and is convinced that her son wishes to put her in a home. Therefore she makes these scenes in public.' She shook her head. 'One day, she will be run over.'

'She nearly was—by me.' Allie was proud of the faint amusement in her voice. 'Luckily, Remy de Brizat came along and calmed her down.'

She waited tensely for Tante's response, but the older woman merely nodded, unfazed. 'He is her doctor, and one of the few people who can deal with her tantrums.'

'I see.' Allie hesitated. 'That—sounds as if he's back for good?' she ventured.

Madelon Colville threaded her needle with care.

'His father hopes so, certainly. The other partner at the medical centre was diagnosed with Parkinson's disease a year ago, and wished to retire, so Remy returned to take his place.' She looked at Allie over the top of her glasses. 'You were surprised to see him, *peut-être*?'

'A little, maybe.' Allie hand-picked her words. 'I guess I—assumed he would still be in Brazil, or wherever the charity had sent him next.'

Tante nodded. 'And you feel, I think, that I should have told you he had come back?'

'No,' Allie said, then, 'Well, maybe. I—I don't know…' She paused. 'Does he know that—I've come back, too?'

'I saw no reason to tell him.' Tante shrugged, her face and voice calm. 'Two years have passed since you parted, *ma chère,* and the world has moved on—as Remy himself has done. He has dismissed the past and come back to resume his life here, just as he should.

'And you also made a decision—to lead your own life in England, with this beautiful child.' Her eyes dwelled thoughtfully on Tom. 'He is the important one now, and that other time, here with Remy, is over and gone, and should be forgotten.'

She paused. 'Besides, he may even be married himself when the summer ends.' She added expressionlessly, 'No doubt you will remember Solange Geran?'

*No doubt…*

The pain was suddenly back, slashing savagely at her, forcing Allie to stifle her involuntary gasp.

'Yes,' she returned steadily. 'Yes, of course I do.'

*How could I possibly forget her—the girl who finally brought my make-believe world crashing in ruins around me?*

*And now—dear God—Remy has come back—to her. I did not bargain for this...*

*And how can I bear it?*

She drank some lemonade, letting the cold tartness trickle over the burning sandpaper that had once been her throat. She made herself sound politely interested. 'Her *gîte* business—is it doing well?'

'It seems that it is. She has converted another barn, and no longer has time to deliver eggs.' Tante set a stitch with minute accuracy. 'Although I had already ceased to buy from her,' she added almost inconsequentially.

Tom was fast approaching again, clutching his ball to his chest. Allie persuaded him to relinquish it, and rolled it again for him to pursue.

She said quietly, 'And now she's going to be a doctor's wife, just as she always wanted.' She forced a smile. 'It's—good that things have worked out so well—for all of us.' She sat up, swallowing the rest of her lemonade. 'And now, maybe, we should talk about you.'

Tante shrugged again. 'I am no longer young. What else is there to say?'

'Quite a bit,' Allie said crisply. 'Are you going to tell me what's wrong? Why you've been seeing the doctor?'

'The ailments of the elderly,' Tante dismissed almost airily. 'So boring to contemplate. So wearying to discuss.'

Allie stared at her. 'It can't be that simple,' she objected. She paused. 'You do realise that your letter implied that you were practically at death's door?'

Tante concentrated on her embroidery. 'As I told you, I have good days and bad days, *ma mie*. I must have written to you on a bad one.'

Allie drew a sharp breath. 'And when Madame Drouac came to look after you—I suppose that was just a bad day too?'

Madame Colville looked faintly mournful. 'All these details—so difficult to remember.'

'Then perhaps I should simply ask your doctor.'

'Ask Remy?' Tante mused. 'I wonder if he would tell you. Or if it would indeed be ethical for him to do so without my permission.'

In the silence that followed, Allie heard herself swallow. She said, 'I—I didn't realise. I thought you were his father's patient.'

'When Dr Varaud left, there was some reassignment.' Tante waved a hand. 'I was happy to consult Remy instead.' She gave a slight cough. 'To reassure you, *ma chère*, I have always found him most kind—most understanding.'

'I'm delighted to hear it.' Allie's tone was wooden. Oh, God, she thought, her stomach churning. If she's under some medical regime, then he may come here. What am I going to do? What can I do?

She leaned forward almost beseechingly. 'Darling, why won't you tell me what the problem is—and how serious? We could always get a second opinion.'

'Because it would change nothing.' There was a finality in Madelon Colville's voice. 'And, believe me, *mon enfant*, I am content for it to be so. In life, at my age, one can only expect the unexpected.' She smiled. 'So, *chérie*, let us simply enjoy this time we have together, *hein*?'

Allie stared at her. Her great-aunt seemed almost tranquil, she thought in unhappy bewilderment. More than that, she'd swear that Madelon even had an air of faint satisfaction. Was that how someone really prepared to relinquish their hold on a good life well lived? She could hardly believe it.

At the same time, it was clear that any expression of sorrow and regret on her own part would not be welcomed. So, in spite of everything, she would have to do her best to remain cheerful and positive.

But at least her concern over Tante might help distance the renewed anguish that hearing about Remy had inevitably evoked.

And the local grapevine worked like a charm, she reminded herself. News of Tante's visitor from England would soon spread. She could only hope that Remy, too, would want no reminder of the betrayal and bitterness of two years before, and take his own avoiding action.

'It's over,' she whispered feverishly to herself. 'And I have to accept that, just as he's done, and deal with it.'

And, at the same time, pray that it's true…

She drew a trembling breath as she reached for Tom as he scurried past and lifted him on to her lap, holding him tightly.

It's your future that matters now, my darling, she told him silently. Your future, and nothing else. And I'll fight tooth and nail to protect it.

# CHAPTER FIVE

THE rest of the day passed slowly. Allie felt constantly on edge, acutely aware of how many topics were necessarily taboo. She was thankful that Tom was there to provide a welcome focus for everyone's attention. His earlier shyness all forgotten, he basked in the unbounded sunshine of approval from Tante and Madame Drouac.

Even so, there were odd pitfalls to be negotiated.

'Amelie says that Thomas has very beautiful eyes,' Tante reported smilingly as Allie came downstairs, slightly damp from an uproarious bath and bedtime session with her son. 'She thinks such an unusual shade of blue.'

'The Marchingtons are all blue-eyed,' Allie returned, rather lamely.

'She feels too that he is most advanced for so young a child,' Madelon Colville added blandly. 'She understood you to say that he has only just passed his first birthday.'

Allie's face warmed. 'I think that may have lost a little in translation,' she said lightly. 'I shall have to work on my French.'

And also watch my step from now on, she added silently. Madame Drouac is clearly nobody's fool.

They spent a quiet evening, preferring to listen to music rather than watch television. But it was not long before Tante announced that she was tired and going to bed.

'And I think you would benefit also from an early night, Alys.'

Allie nodded. 'I'll be up soon.'

But when the Chopin *nocturne* ended, she slid Debussy's *'Prelude à l'après midi d'un faune'* into the CD player, and settled back against the cushions to listen, allowing the music to recapture for her all the drowsy, languid warmth of a magical afternoon. A time when anything could happen.

Like that first afternoon with Remy, she thought, a fist clenching in her stomach. Never to be forgotten.

She'd sat tautly beside him in his Jeep, she remembered, her hands gripped together in her lap, staring through the windscreen without absorbing much. Conscious only of the man beside her.

'Relax, Alys,' he had commanded softly. 'Or you will make me nervous too.'

'Not much chance of that,' she muttered.

'No?' There was amusement in his voice. 'You would be surprised. But you will feel better, perhaps, when you have had something to eat.'

'It's not always a question of blood sugar levels, *monsieur le docteur*,' she countered. She shook her head. 'I still don't know why I'm doing this.'

'I hi-jacked you, *chérie*,' he said cheerfully. 'I like to look at something beautiful during my mealtimes.'

Her brows lifted. 'Really? I thought most Frenchmen preferred to look at what was on their plates.'

'Then you know very little about Frenchmen.'

'And,' she said, 'believe it or not, I was perfectly happy in my ignorance.'

He burst out laughing. 'One day, *ma mie*,' he said, 'I shall remind you of that.' He turned the Jeep off the narrow coast road they'd been following, and drove inland along a rough track towards a circle of standing stones silhouetted against the horizon.

'Don't tell me,' Allie commented brightly as he brought the vehicle to a halt. 'This used to be a place for human sacrifice, and I'm the main course.'

Remy grinned at her. 'Legend says that they were all bad girls from nearby villages, lured here by a local saint in the guise of a handsome young man, who turned them to stone when they refused to repent their wicked ways.' He took a rug from the back of the Jeep and tossed it to her. 'Maybe a sacrifice would have been kinder.'

'And the *men* who weren't saints?' she enquired tartly, as he lifted out a hamper. 'Who'd contributed to the girls' downfall? I suppose they got off scot-free?'

'That might depend, *ma belle*, on whether or not they were found out by their wives.'

Allie gave him a cold look and followed him, holding the rug against her as if it provided some kind of defence.

They walked through the stones and down into a small sheltered hollow, where Remy spread the rug on the short grass and began to unpack the basket. Allie stationed herself at a distance and watched. It was, she reflected, quite a sophisticated performance, with covered pottery dishes, gleaming silverware, a white linen cloth, and crystal glasses wrapped in matching napkins. Not a plastic spoon or limp sandwich in sight. And a means to an end if ever she'd seen one.

Seduction-by-Sea, she told herself wryly. And I wonder how many other girls he's brought to this same secluded spot?

On the other hand, what could it possibly matter? He was here with her for the first time and the last, and whatever plans he might have for post-prandial entertainment were doomed to disappointment.

Unless, of course, he decided to use force…

For a brief moment something cold and dead lodged like a stone within her, and was immediately dismissed.

No, she thought, he would never do that. Because he would never have to. There would be no lack of willing women in his life. Enough, probably, to embellish the whole of Finistere with stone circles if truth be told.

'You look very fierce, Alys,' he commented. 'Calm yourself with some pâté. It has come from the Inter-marche, so it is quite safe.'

Allie, remembering what Tante had said about the cooking at Trehel, was betrayed into a giggle.

'Ah,' he said. 'I see poor Liliane's fame has reached

Les Sables. And yet as a housekeeper she is—*formidable*. No speck of grime is allowed to exist. *Mais, malheureusement*, the food is also massacred.' He shook his head. 'We try—my grandfather, my father and I—to keep her from the stove, but at the same time we do not wish to hurt her feelings. She is a kind soul.'

The pâté *was* good, she discovered, as were the thick slices of ham, the chunks of smoked sausage, and the sliced duck breast that followed. To accompany the crusty *baguette* there was a slab of butter in a refrigerated dish, and a creamy local cheese, wrapped in a checked cloth.

The wine Remy poured for them both was pale and crisp, but she was told there was also mineral water, if she preferred.

She decided to risk the wine, sipping circumspectly, and if he noticed her restraint he made no comment.

To complete the meal there were strawberries, in a bowl lined with green leaves.

Allie pushed her plate away with a little sigh of repletion. 'That was—delicious.'

'And I am forgiven for having kidnapped you?'

'I'll overlook it,' she said. 'This once.'

He smiled at her lazily. 'I hope it will never again be necessary.' He paused. 'I regret there is no coffee, but I think it should be made and drunk while it is fresh. Although, being English, you drink only tea, perhaps?'

'Not at all,' she said. 'Besides, my grandmother was French, don't forget.'

'The Vaillac sisters.' He began to put the used things

back in the hamper. 'My grandfather knew them as young girls, and says they were both beauties.' He paused. 'He was surprised, I think, when Madame Colville decided to return. And pleased, too. He says it is good to come back to the place where you were born. So many—just leave.'

He put the hamper to one side and refilled their glasses. 'He says also that this is not your first visit. That you came here with your father while I was working abroad.'

'Yes, I did,' she said. 'More than once.' She paused. 'Which makes my idiotic behaviour on the beach the other morning even more unforgivable. I—should have known better.'

'And I,' he said, 'could have been kinder.'

He had moved closer, she realised suddenly, and his hand was only a couple of inches from hers. She looked down at the long fingers with their short, well-kept nails, and remembered how they'd felt, touching her skin. A tiny flame of forbidden excitement sprang into life deep within her, and had to be suppressed.

She hurried to fill the silence. 'You speak marvellous English.' *Oh, God, I sound all eager and—girly.*

He shrugged. 'When I qualified, I worked in Britain for a while. Also America. And when I was employed by the charity English was the common language too. So now, of course, I am given the tourists to deal with at the medical centre.'

'Yes,' she said. 'Of course. Well, I'll—try to lessen your workload and not get sick.'

His mouth quirked. 'You are all consideration, *ma mie*, but you seem to be in good health. You are still pale, of course.' His hand closed round her wrist. 'And your pulse is too rapid,' he added softly. 'But I do not think the symptoms are dangerous.'

Oh, but you're wrong—so wrong, she thought wildly. Because I've never been in such danger before. Never...

She glanced down, realising that his fingers were entwined with hers now, and that somehow his other arm was encircling her shoulders. She felt his cheek against her hair. Became aware that he was lifting her hand, brushing her knuckles gently with his lips, then turning it to press a kiss into the centre of her palm. It was the briefest of caresses. Yet she felt it jolt through her entire body like an electric charge.

And heard herself whisper desperately, 'No—please. No.'

He released her instantly, but he did not move away from her. She could feel the warmth of him through her thin shirt. He said quietly, 'No to a kiss, *ma belle*? Or—no, I may not undress you, as I so much wish to do, and make love to you here in the sunlight?'

'No to any of it. All of it.' She stumbled over the words. 'You mustn't... I can't...' She added desperately, 'Please take me home.'

There was a silence, thoughtful rather than laced with the anger she'd expected.

He stroked her cheek, then smoothed her hair back behind her ear, his thumb gently brushing the lobe. He said softly, 'Are you a virgin, Alys?'

She stared wildly in front of her, not daring to turn her head and meet his gaze. She said huskily, 'You have no right to ask me that.'

'You think not? But between lovers it is a matter of some importance.'

'We are—not lovers.' Her tone had become a croak.

'Not yet, perhaps. But one day—one night soon—it will happen.' He added levelly, 'As you know well, Alys. So do not let us pretend any longer, or play games with words. It follows that I need to know if you are truly as inexperienced as you seem.'

She still could not look at him. She spoke reluctantly, stumbling a little. 'Then—no. I've had sex—before.'

'Ah,' he said meditatively. 'You do not appear to recall it with pleasure.'

She bit her lip. 'It was at a college party,' she said at last. 'In an empty bedroom with someone who'd never paid me much attention before. And nothing really changed, because it was awkward, uncomfortable, and thankfully over very quickly.' She tried to smile. 'Afterwards, I wanted to die of embarrassment. My only excuse, and I'm not proud of it, is that I'd had too much to drink.'

*And I've never told anyone before—so why now? Oh, God, why you…?*

'What a terrible confession,' Remy said, after a pause. He reached for the bottle and held it out to her. 'Have some more wine.'

She gasped indignantly, turning on him, then halted. How could she have ever thought his eyes were cold?

she asked herself dazedly. They were so alive and brilliant with laughter, mingled with something that might almost have been tenderness.

She mumbled, 'It's not funny.'

'No,' he said. 'It is not.' He poured the rest of the wine on to the grass, and returned the empty bottle to the basket.

He said softly, 'Let me tell you something, *chérie*. A man who chooses to make love to a girl when her senses are dulled with alcohol is a fool. When you come to me, Alys, I promise you will know exactly what you are doing at every moment.'

Her heart was battering her ribcage. She said thickly, 'It will never happen.'

His brows lifted. 'You doubt my resolve, Alys? *Eh, bien…*'

He reached for her almost casually, pulling her against him so that she was lying across his body. Then he bent his head, and his mouth took hers—slowly, but very surely.

She knew she should resist. The need to do so was imperative. Absolute. But she had no defence against the warm, mesmerising power of his kiss. And the complete absence of any kind of pressure was her undoing. His lips moved on hers with a tantalising gentleness wholly outside her experience. The tip of his tongue probed softly, coaxing her to open to him. To allow the caressing mouth to take her to a new and more sensuous level.

Almost imperceptibly Allie found her body relaxing against his, her breathing quickening unevenly as she yielded to the intimate exploration of the inner contours of her mouth, the delicate, provocative play of his tongue against hers.

And when at last he raised his head and looked down at her, the blue eyes grave and questioning, she breathed, 'Remy,' on a little sigh, and her arms went round his neck to draw him back to her again.

At once his kiss deepened, hardening into a new dimension of heated possession, and Allie responded passionately to his demands, her own mouth as eager—as seeking.

The blood seared her veins as she clung to him, her fingers gripping the strength of bone and muscles in his shoulders through the thin shirt as she tasted—breathed with desire—the erotic male scent of him.

His hand lifted to cup her breast, his thumb stroking its tender peak slowly and rhythmically, teasing it to quivering arousal until she moaned softly into his mouth, her body arching towards him.

Hunger was burning her now—melting her with the first real discovery of her own female physicality. Making her aware of the scalding rush between her thighs. Rendering her defenceless against whatever he might ask of her.

Slowly, almost lingeringly Remy took his mouth from hers, his hand from her body. Even moved back a little, pushing his hair from his face.

She looked up at him, her eyes half closed, drowsy with need as she began one by one to unfasten the buttons on her shirt. To offer herself.

Only to find his hand closing round hers, halting her.

He said huskily, his breathing ragged, 'You taste of strawberries and wine, Alys.' He paused, shaking his head almost dazedly. 'But now I think—I know—that I should take you home.'

'But I thought…' The stumbling words were out before she could prevent them, their bewildered message unmistakable.

Oh, God, she thought, shamed to the bone. I'm pleading with him for sex when he's already turned me down. Please—this can't be happening to me.

Words slunk from the past to haunt her. *Useless— stupid—frigid…* All the taunts, the accusations, coming home to roost. Branding her for ever with their terrible truth.

Shocked blood rushed to her face as she realised, too, what she must look like, dazed with desire, her hardened nipples thrusting against the cling of her di- shevelled blouse. Stunned, she scrambled away from him, clumsy in her haste. 'Yes—yes, of course. I—I'm sorry. We should go. Tante will wonder…'

And then the words ran out on a little gasp, and she could only put her hands over her face, unable to bear the renewed humiliation of seeing the pity in his eyes when he looked at her.

Remy said something half under his breath, and his hands clamped firmly round her wrists, tugging them away.

'You think, maybe, that I do not want you?' The question was almost harsh. 'But you are so wrong,

Alys. I hesitate only because I do not wish you to think I am like that other man. That I ask only for the pleasure of the moment. For us, that can never be the choice, and we both know it. There must be more between us than just a meeting of bodies.'

'Then—what?' Somehow, Allie forced the question from trembling lips.

He sighed. 'I think that I need you to trust me, *mon ange*.'

'I do.' Her protest was swift.

'But not enough. Believe me.' His tone was quiet but forceful. He cupped her face between his hands, the blue eyes intense. 'How can you, when you hardly know me? When we hardly know each other?' He shrugged, his smile crooked. 'So—that must change. And I—I will have to learn patience.'

'So will I.' Her admission was shy. She turned her head, pressing a kiss into the warmth of his palm.

'Ah, *mon coeur*.' He took her back into his arms, holding her close for a few heart-stopping moments, releasing her with open reluctance. 'We had better go now,' he muttered roughly. 'Before I am tempted beyond endurance.'

Allie's glance through her lashes was mischievous as he helped her to her feet. 'Isn't that why you brought me here in the first place?'

'Of course.' His mouth twisted ruefully. 'But I am only human, Alys, and therefore allowed to hope—being no saint.'

'I'm glad.' She glanced round at the standing

stones. 'The local variety took a tough line with straying girls. Maybe he could have used a little humanity too.'

'Perhaps we were right not to risk his anger?' Remy suggested. Then, as she turned away, he halted her. 'Wait, *ma mie*, I need to tidy you a little.' She obeyed, standing demurely while Remy carefully rebuttoned her gaping shirt and brushed tell-tale fronds of dried grass from her clothes and hair.

'But I can do nothing about your eyes, *chérie*, or your beautiful mouth,' he added huskily. 'You look entirely like a girl who has been in the arms of her lover. I only hope your great-aunt does not bar me from her house.'

*She won't do that.* The words remained on her lips, unsaid, as she suddenly realised, with a kind of shock, that she could guarantee no such thing. Tante Madelon was a woman of another generation entirely, with strict views on marriage and its obligations, even when it was clearly as ill-advised and wretched as Allie's was.

And as it would remain.

Because, all too soon, this brief respite would be over, and she would have to go back. Back to the misery of emptiness and blame.

She glanced sideways at him as they drove away, thinking of the strength of the arms that had held her, the grace of his mouth. Feeling her starving body clench in a swift, primitive craving that screamed out for the ultimate fulfilment.

She'd denied herself a normal life, she thought desperately, trying to appease her conscience. Surely she was entitled to some happiness—just for a while—wasn't she? A little sweetness to comfort her in the barren time ahead? Was it really so much to ask?

She saw, in the wing mirror, the image of the stone circle, pointing grimly, like so many warning fingers, towards the sky. And realised, as her heart skipped a beat, that her question had been answered.

To hell with it, she told the unseen forces of retribution. I won't give him up. Not yet. Because I can't. And if there's a price to pay, then I'll just have to face that when it happens.

They said little on the way back to Les Sables. The road ahead was empty, and Remy took one hand from the wheel, clasping her fingers lightly as they drove.

So this is first love, she thought, turning to feast her eyes on him. Come to me at last.

And she saw his mouth slant in a swift smile, as if he'd read her thoughts.

As they drove up to the house, Tante emerged, and stood waiting for them. Her face was tranquil as she watched Remy go round to the passenger door and help her great-niece, very circumspectly, to alight, but Allie was not deceived.

She's probably been pacing the rug since we left, she thought with a sigh.

Remy must have sensed the same thing, because he said, with a touch of dryness, 'As you see, I have returned her safely, *madame.*'

She picked up his tone. '*Mon cher* Remy, I never

doubted you for an instant.' She paused. 'May I offer you some coffee before you depart?'

'*Merci, madame*, but I think I must get back to Trehel. I have some matters to discuss with the builders.' He made her a small polite bow, then turned to Allie, his face smooth, but little devils glinting in his eyes. '*Au revoir*, Alys. I hope you will permit me to call on you again?'

She looked down at her feet. 'Why, yes. Thank you. If you wish. That would be—very nice,' she added wildly.

'Then I too shall look forward to it.' There was only the slightest tremor in his voice, but the wickedly prim face he pulled at her as he walked towards the Jeep was almost her undoing.

As he reached it, another vehicle—a blue pick-up—suddenly pulled in behind him with a crackling swirl of gravel. The driver's door was flung wide, and a girl jumped down.

She was small, with silver-blonde hair and a pretty heart-shaped face, all huge brown eyes, and a sexy mouth painted bright pink, with her finger and toenails enamelled to match.

She possessed a shapely figure bordering on the frankly voluptuous, set off by tight white trousers and a scoop-necked top in a stinging shade of violet. And she was smiling widely as she ran across to Remy and kissed him on both cheeks, standing charmingly on tiptoe in order to do so.

'*Chéri.*' She had a soft, throaty voice. 'I thought I

recognised your Jeep. But why are you here?' She turned to Madelon. 'Please tell me you are not ill, *ma chère madame*.'

'Not in the least,' said Tante briskly. 'Dr de Brizat has been kind enough to show my great-niece from England something of the surrounding area. That is all.'

'You, Remy? Turned tour guide?' The newcomer gurgled with laughter. '*Mon Dieu*, the world will end tomorrow. And I thought your every moment outside work was spent either with Roland or on the renovations at Trehel.'

'Not every moment,' Remy returned coolly. 'I allow myself some leisure—from time to time.'

Her eyes widened extravagantly in a way that Allie decided must have taken hours of practice. 'Then your friends can hope to see more of you, maybe? What a pleasure that will be.'

She turned to Allie, her gaze flickering over her. A glance that assessed and dismissed. 'So—an English visitor.' She made it sound as if the other girl had escaped from a zoo. 'Then we must all do what we can to ensure that you enjoy your vacation—*Mademoiselle*...?' She paused questioningly.

'Alys,' Remy supplied quietly. 'Alys Colville.'

'*Enchantée*. And I am Solange Geran.' The smile flashed again, but the brown eyes were watchful. 'I am sure we shall become friends. You intend to remain for a long time with *madame*, I hope.'

Under the gush, the message reached Allie loud and clear.

She considers me no contest, she thought. But, all the same, she'd be delighted to hear that I'm leaving tomorrow.

She shrugged gracefully. 'My plans are—fluid at the moment.'

'But mine, unfortunately, are not,' Remy said briskly. 'So, forgive me, but I must go.' As he swung himself into the Jeep he looked briefly across at Allie, his lips miming a swift kiss before driving away.

'*Alors*, I must find my purse,' Madelon Colville said as the noise of the engine faded. 'I presume you have brought the eggs, Solange?'

Solange was looking at the road, her lower lip held in her teeth, but when she turned back she was dimpling. 'But of course. *Une douzaine, madame, comme d'habitude.*'

'Then bring them inside, if you will,' Tante directed. 'Come, Alys, and help me with the coffee.

'Solange's parents bought the farm from me,' she added in an undertone as she led the way into the house. 'But when her late father's health began to fail she took a government grant and began converting the barns and outbuildings into *gîtes*, which have been a great success. The egg business is now merely a sideline, but at least it enables her to get away from Ravac.'

She pursed her lips. 'Since she was widowed, Madame Geran has become something of a trial, I understand.'

Allie understood too. We could almost start a company, she thought. Difficult Widows R Us.

She said shortly, 'Solange has my sympathy.'

Tante gave her an ironic look. 'I doubt, *mon enfant*, that she would welcome it. Do you?'

It was an awkward little interlude. Solange arrived with the eggs, and accepted her cup of coffee with pretty thanks. Sitting at the table, listening to her chat away to Tante, Allie was aware that she was being covertly studied, and with no friendly eye.

And until a short while ago, *mademoiselle*, I didn't know you existed either, she told the other girl silently.

Solange was amusing about the problems of running *gîtes*, especially Allie noted, where English guests were concerned. Their eccentricities, messy habits, and petty meannesses were dwelt on with particular relish. But her other main topic was Trehel, and the barn there that Remy was converting into a house for his own occupation.

'It has taken so long, he is almost in despair,' she confided. She sighed portentously. 'But he would employ Gaston Levecq, in spite of all our warnings.'

'The Levecqs lost their youngest child to meningitis,' said Tante. 'And *madame* suffered terribly with depression afterwards. Remy may have felt Gaston needed the distraction of a new project. And he is a good workman.'

'Oh, I agree that it is going to be beautiful. All the top floor is finished now, and the view from the main bedroom is *formidable*.' Solange played coyly with the handle of her coffee cup. 'Remy has asked me to help with the décor, you understand?'

She drank the remains of her coffee and rose. 'And now I must deliver the rest of the eggs,' she announced brightly. 'People will be wondering where I am.'

After she left, there was silence. Then Allie said, her smile forced, 'I think I've just been warned off her territory.'

Tante's voice was troubled. '*Mon enfant*—when you have gone back to your own life, she will still be here, and Remy too. Are you being quite fair?'

Allie bent her head. 'Tante—please don't ask me not to see him again, because I don't think that's possible.'

Madelon Colville gave a heavy sigh. '*Mon Dieu*,' she said, half to herself. 'Has it already gone so far and so fast?'

Colour rose in Allie's face. 'No,' she protested. 'Nothing's—happened.'

Her great-aunt's brows lifted. 'Nothing? You mean, *en effet*, that you have not yet given yourself to him?' Her little shrug was a masterpiece of Gallic cynicism. 'Well, it is only a matter of time. Every word that was spoken—every look—proclaimed that.'

'But we didn't…'

'Precisely.' Madame Colville nodded grimly. 'Alys— I say this only from love. It might be better for you to go now. Leave Brittany before real damage is done.'

Allie looked at her across the table, sudden tears hanging from her lashes. She said, 'I don't think I can.' And her voice broke.

# CHAPTER SIX

ALLIE got up early the next morning. She pulled on shorts and a tee-shirt, and let herself quietly out of the house. She didn't go down to the beach, but walked along the top of the cliff until she reached a patch of grass, where she sat. She turned her face to the sun while the fresh sea breeze lifted the strands of her light brown hair, letting the cloud of Tante's anxiety which had hung over her since the previous day dissipate, while her heart thudded in eager anticipation.

She did not have to wait long before she was aware of Roland's hoofbeats, quiet on the short turf, and horse and rider dark against the pale morning sky.

He said softly, 'I knew you would be here.' He reached down a hand, pulling her up on to the saddle in front of him. Settling her carefully.

'Won't Roland mind?' She ran a hand over the glossy mane.

'He will have to accustom himself.' As they moved off, he said, 'Is there anything you wish to ask me, *ma belle*? Anything you need to know?'

'No.' His arms around her conveyed all the lovely

certainty she needed. She found herself thinking *Poor Solange*, then added aloud, 'Unless you have something you want to say to me?'

'Many things.' He pushed up the sleeve of her tee-shirt and kissed her bare shoulder, his lips warm and lingering against her cool skin. 'But they will have to wait.'

'Where are we going?'

'To have breakfast,' he said. 'At Trehel.'

'Oh,' she said, a touch doubtfully. 'Your family won't mind?'

His lips touched her hair. 'They will have to accustom themselves also.'

'But how will I get back?'

'Naturally I shall drive you home, before I go into Ignac. Or did you think I would send you back on Roland?'

'It crossed my mind,' she admitted, and heard him laugh softly.

They were quiet for a while, then she said, 'Do you know this is only my second time on the back of a horse?'

'*Vraiment?* I hope you are a little more comfortable this time. And that you do not find it as frightening.'

'Oh, I'm still a little scared,' she said. 'But for very different reasons.'

'Ah, *mon ange*.' His voice was gentle. 'Alys, you must know that I would never willingly do anything to hurt you.'

*Or I you. Never willingly. But I know in my heart that I shall—because I can't help myself...*

Perhaps their need for each other would be like a summer storm, she thought with sudden sadness. Raging for a while, then blowing itself out, with no lasting harm in its wake. Maybe even enabling them to say goodbye as friends.

'*Qu'as-tu*, Alys?' He must have sensed her disquiet. 'Is something the matter?'

'No, nothing. Except—I was thinking how strange life is. How unexpected.'

'You think so?' She heard the smile in his voice. 'Yet I know I have been waiting for you since the day I was born. Is it not the same for you?'

'Yes,' she told him quietly. 'Oh, yes.'

And knew, with sadness, that she spoke only the truth. But that it was all, tragically, too late…

Trehel was an old grey stone house, massive among its surrounding grasslands and trees, with three storeys of shuttered windows that seemed to be watching like half-closed eyes as they rode up. Allie could only hope the scrutiny was friendly.

Remy walked Roland round the side of the house to a large courtyard holding stables and outbuildings.

There was a big barn set well back from the yard, and Allie could hear the noise of sawing and hammering emanating from it.

'Is that where you're planning to live?' she asked as Remy dismounted and lifted her down.

'Yes,' he said, then looked at her, his mouth twisting

ruefully. 'Ah, Solange must have told you. What else did she say?'

Allie shrugged. 'That it hadn't gone entirely to plan.' *Also, she happened to mention the view from the bedroom.*

'The building work has been more slow than I had hoped,' he admitted. 'However, it should be finished soon.'

'May I see round it?'

'Of course, but not now,' he said, tossing Roland's reins to the elderly man emerging from the stables. He added softly, 'One day, *ma belle*, when we have more time.' And the promise in his voice warmed her skin.

Then he took her hand, and led her into the house.

She found herself in a huge kitchen, with a long table at its centre. A tall white-haired man was busying himself at the range with a kettle as they came in, and the two dogs of indeterminate breed who were lying beside him looked up, thumped feathery tails on the rug, then relapsed into doing very little again.

The man turned, and Allie found herself being studied by shrewd blue eyes under bushy eyebrows.

He said, 'So, Remy, who is this lovely girl you have brought to brighten our morning?'

'I wish you to meet Alys, Grandpère. She is Celine Vaillac's granddaughter. *Ma mie*, this is my grandfather, Georges de Brizat.'

'But of course.' The rather stern mouth softened into a warm smile. 'I was foolish not to have known at once. You are very like her, *mademoiselle*.'

And you, she thought. One look at you, and I know exactly what Remy will be like as he grows old.

And she felt pain slash at her as she realised she would not be there to see him…

Oh, God, she thought, this is all so wrong. I shouldn't even be here now. The whole situation's getting out of hand.

But she recovered herself instantly, shook hands, murmuring a polite greeting, and sat at the table to be served with warm rolls, cherry jam, and large bowls of hot chocolate.

'Where is Papa?' Remy asked.

'The Richaud baby. They telephoned at dawn after the first contraction, I think.'

'Well, it is understandable,' Remy said tolerantly. 'After four girls, Richaud is desperate for a boy.' He grinned. 'It has become a matter of public concern, Alys. They have been laying odds in the Café des Sports.'

Her mouth was suddenly bone-dry. 'Poor woman— to have so much expected of her,' she managed, and gulped some of her chocolate.

Georges de Brizat came and sat at the head of the table, followed hopefully by the dogs. He gave Allie another thoughtful look. 'You are staying with Madame Colville, *mademoiselle*? She is well, I hope.'

'Absolutely fine.' She forced a smile.

'Good.' His nod was faintly abstracted. 'Good. You will tell her I was asking about her? Also, give her my best wishes?'

'Yes—yes, of course.'

'We knew each other many years ago, during the bad years of the Occupation. She and her sister were brave girls. Brave and very beautiful.' He paused. 'They had happy lives—with their Englishmen?'

'Yes,' Allie returned, faintly surprised. 'Very happy.'

He nodded again, then applied himself to his breakfast.

One of the dogs came and laid a chin on her leg, and she stroked his silky head and fondled his ears, before slipping him a morsel of bread and jam, while Remy watched her with such tender amusement that she wanted to get up from her chair, and go round the table into his arms, to remain there for ever.

But he was getting briskly to his feet. 'I must go and shower. Get ready for work.' As he passed his grandfather's chair, he dropped a hand on the old man's shoulder. 'Be gentle with Alys, Grandpère. No Resistance-style interrogation, *s'il te plaît*.'

When they were alone, Dr de Brizat cleared his throat. 'Remy likes his joke, Mademoiselle Alys. But a beautiful girl at the breakfast table is a rarity in this house, so I am bound to be intrigued. How did you meet my grandson?'

Allie carefully added butter and jam to her remaining fragment of roll. 'I was on the beach below Les Sables. Remy warned me about the tide, but I stupidly took no notice, so he—came back for me.'

'He behaved with great wisdom,' said his grandfather. 'You are planning a lengthy visit to Madame Colville?'

She flushed. 'I'm not altogether sure of my plans—at the moment.'

She was bracing herself for more questions, when the rear door opened, and a voice called, 'Remy? *Tu es là?*' Solange Geran walked into the kitchen. She presented a more muted appearance this morning, in denim jeans and a matching shirt, her hair pulled back from her face.

She checked when she saw Allie, looking thunderstruck. 'You?' Her tone was less than friendly. 'What are you doing here?'

Georges de Brizat got politely to his feet. '*Bonjour*, Solange. As you see, we have a guest for breakfast.' He added mildly, 'I hope you have no objection?'

'Why, no. I mean—how could I?' The girl gave a swift trill of laughter. 'How absurd. It was just—a surprise to see Mademoiselle Colville again—so soon.' She glanced around. 'But where is Remy?'

'Taking a shower,' his grandfather returned. 'May I pass on some message?'

'No, thank you.'

'You are quite sure? It must have been a matter of some urgency to bring you here at such an hour.'

The pretty mouth was sulky. 'It is my mother,' she said. 'The trouble with her knee. She complains that she hardly slept last night. I hoped that Remy would call at the farm on his way to Ignac.'

'I regret that will not be possible, as he will be driving Mademoiselle Alys to Les Sables before going to work.' He added tranquilly, 'But if you bring your mother to the medical centre later in the morning, he can examine her there.'

'Since my father's death, my mother rarely leaves the house.'

Monsieur de Brizat shrugged. 'Then, instead, I will request my son to pay her a visit once he returns from the Richauds'.' His tone was dry. 'He used to attend *madame*, so he is well acquainted with the case.'

In spite of her embarrassment, Allie had to stifle a giggle. Game, set and match to Dr Georges, she thought.

Solange's face was like a mask. She said stiffly, 'That is—kind. I shall tell Maman to expect him.'

*'D'accord.'* He waited for a moment as she stood irresolute. 'There was something else, perhaps?'

'No, no.' It was Solange's turn to shrug. 'At least— just a matter of some curtain fabric. But that can wait for another time. When Remy is not quite so—occupied.' She looked at Allie, a faintly metallic note creeping into her voice. *'Au revoir, mademoiselle.* I am sure we shall meet again—soon.'

'I look forward to it,' Allie responded, without an atom of sincerity.

A thoughtful silence followed Solange's departure.

Allie drew a breath. 'I seem to be in the middle of some kind of situation here. Please believe I—I didn't know.'

'You are sure there is anything to know?' Dr de Brizat sighed a little. 'Like all the Gerans, Solange is industrious, ambitious, and single-minded. She has a mother who is a trial, and she does not intend to spend her entire life cleaning cottages for tourists.' He paused. 'But any plans she is making for the future are hers alone.'

His sudden smile was mischievous. 'Let me assure you also, *ma petite*, that she has never been asked to breakfast.'

But that, thought Allie, reluctantly returning his smile, does not make me feel any better about all this.

Remy came striding in, tucking a grey and white striped shirt into charcoal pants, his dark hair still damp from the shower.

Allie was sharply aware of the scent of soap he brought with him, mixed with the faint fragrance of some musky aftershave, and was ashamed to feel her body clench in sheer longing.

He snatched car keys from a bowl on the huge built-in dresser that filled one wall, then reached for Allie's hand, pulling her to her feet. *'Viens, chérie.'*

She managed to throw a hasty *au revoir* over her shoulder to his grandfather, and heard him reply, '*A bientôt*, Mademoiselle Alys.' Which meant that he expected to see her again, she thought, as Remy whisked her into the Jeep and started the engine.

She said breathlessly, 'Do you live your entire life at this speed?'

'No.' The smile he slanted at her was wicked. 'There are times, *mon ange*, when I like to take things very slowly indeed. You would like me to demonstrate?'

'Not,' she said, struggling not to laugh, 'in a moving Jeep, *monsieur, je t'en prie*.'

He gave an exaggerated sigh. *'Eh, bien, chérie, tu as raison, peut-être.'*

There was a brief silence, and when he spoke again his voice was quiet and infinitely serious, 'But I am beginning to question, Alys, how long I can exist without you, and that is the truth.'

She felt a tide of heat sweep through her body, leaving behind it an ache beyond remedy. 'Remy— this isn't easy for me.'

'And you think it is for me?' His laugh was almost bitter. 'That I expected to feel like this—to know how completely my life has changed in so short a time? That I even wished it, when a few days ago I was not even aware of your existence? No, *mon amour,* and no.'

The passion in his tone almost scared her, and Allie bent her head. She said half to herself, 'Oh, God, I shouldn't have come here…'

'Do not say so.' His voice hardened. 'Do not ever say that, *mon coeur*, because without you I would be only half alive.'

He reached out a hand, resting it on her bare leg, just above the knee, and she covered it with both her own, feeling the reassurance of its warmth as they drove in silence back to Les Sables.

When they reached the house, Remy switched off the engine, then turned to her, drawing her into his arms. He looked down at her for a long moment, before taking her mouth with his, kissing her with a thoroughness and frank expertise that left her dizzied and gasping for breath, her hands clutching the front of his shirt as if it was her last hold on sanity.

'Remy…' His name was a croak.

'I need the taste of you, *mon ange*.' His own breathing was ragged. 'To carry with me through the day.' He detached one of the clinging hands and carried it to his lips. 'I will see you tonight? You will have dinner with me?'

She nodded almost numbly, then got out of the Jeep, shading her eyes from the morning sun as she watched him drive away.

Tante was sitting at the kitchen table, reading her letters, as Allie came into the house. Her calm gaze assimilated the dishevelled hair, the wild rose flush and the faintly swollen mouth, but she made no comment.

'The coffee is fresh, dear child, if you would like some.'

'I—I had breakfast at Trehel.'

The older woman nodded drily. 'So Georges de Brizat told me on the telephone.' She paused. 'Your little web of untruth is spreading dangerously wide, *ma mie*. How long before it breaks, I ask myself?'

Allie sat down at the table, staring down at the oilcloth, tracing its pattern with a finger. She said in a low voice, 'I know I have to tell him, Tante Madelon, and I will—soon. I promise. But…'

'But you are so happy you cannot bear anything that might spoil your idyll.' Tante studied her. 'You do not trust Remy to understand?'

'I—I'm learning to trust.'

'Then learn quickly, *ma chère*.' Tante got briskly to her feet and fetched the coffee from the stove. 'Before he guesses you are hiding something—and begins to wonder if he can trust *you*.'

I should have listened to her, Allie thought wretchedly, sitting up and easing her back, stiff from sitting so long in one position on the sofa. I should have taken the risk and told Remy everything. But I was too scared of losing him. And in the end, because I was stupid and a coward, I lost him anyway...

The music had ended long ago, and she replaced the CD in its case and switched off the player.

The house was totally silent, the blackness of the night pressing against the windows, making her feel suddenly isolated—alienated.

She thought with a shiver, It's very late. I should go to bed, instead of tormenting myself with the desperation of the past.

Because Remy won't be listening to the silence, or staring into the darkness a few miles away at Trehel. He's not torturing himself with bad memories. He's put the past where it belongs and set his life back in order, the way it should always have been.

So, he'll be asleep in that enormous bed, with Solange in his arms, her bright sunflower hair across his pillow and that little victorious smile on her lips.

Solange...

Jerkily, she brought her clenched fist to her mouth. Bit savagely at the knuckle as pain ravaged her.

Solange, she thought, wincing. The girl she'd seen as an irritant, perhaps, but never a danger. Someone she'd underestimated from Day One—that she'd even allowed herself to pity a little. But perhaps her happiness with Remy had made her blind—even arrogant.

She opened the back door and stood leaning against the frame, drawing in deep lungfuls of cool air as she fought for calm.

Because she had been happy in a way that was totally outside her experience, measuring her life only in the hours they spent together. Beginning with the dinner he'd promised her that evening...

'Richaud has a son at last,' he'd told her with amusement, as they'd sat eating lobster in a candlelit restaurant overlooking the sea. 'Papa says he will be drunk for a week in celebration.'

Allie dealt carefully with a claw. 'Is it really so important to men—this need for a male heir?'

He shrugged. 'The inheritance laws are different here, but a son at least carries on the family name, and for Richaud it also means a strong arm to help him on his land.' He looked at her, brows lifted. 'You think that is a chauvinist point of view, *ma belle*?'

'I suppose not,' she said. 'As long as it doesn't become an obsession.'

'Your father would have preferred a son?' He smiled at her. 'That I do not believe.' He paused. 'For myself, a healthy child born safely to the woman I love is all I would ever want.'

*Now*, whispered the voice in her head. *Be honest with him. Tell him about Hugo—the nightmare of your marriage. Tell him everything—now—and ask for his understanding—his help...*

But as she nerved herself the waiter appeared beside them, pouring more wine, whisking away the discarded pieces of shell, and the moment was lost.

And when they arrived back at Les Sables, Tante was waiting up, hiding her private concerns behind polite welcome, but clearly determined not to leave them alone together.

Remy's goodnight kiss was frankly rueful. 'Tomorrow,' he whispered. 'I am free in the afternoon. Will you come swimming with me?'

'Yes.' Allie's eyes shone as she detached herself reluctantly from his arms. 'Yes, of course.'

'We have a pool at Trehel, but I think *madame* would feel that is too secluded.' He paused. 'So, to assure her of my good intentions, I shall take you to St Calot, where there will be many other people.'

She bit her lip. 'Remy—she really likes you...'

His tone was wry. 'Yet she still looks at me, *mon ange*, as if I were a wolf, threatening her only lamb.' He sighed. 'However, she is right to care about you. And I have only to persuade her that I care too.' He kissed her again. '*A demain.*'

Except it's not you, but me that she doesn't trust, Allie thought with sudden bleakness as she turned back into the house. And I can't blame her for that.

* * *

The weather continued to be glorious, with each sunlit tomorrow blending seamlessly into the next, and Remy making time to be with her on each of them, in spite of his workload.

But as the days passed Allie found the idea of sharing the truth with him was becoming ever more difficult. She felt totally detached from her previous life, as if Marchington Hall existed on some other planet, and the sole reality was here and now, with the man she loved and wanted so passionately.

'I am going to Vannes tomorrow, to visit some old friends,' Tante announced one evening. She added drily, 'I take it that you will not wish to go with me?'

Allie flushed. 'I'd rather stay here—if you don't mind.'

'*Au contraire, chérie.* I suspect you would not have an enlivening day with Emil and Annette. And I am also sure you will not be lonely.' She paused. 'I do not condone, but I understand, *ma chère*,' she added quietly, 'and I simply—bow to the inevitable.'

There was a silence, then Allie said huskily, 'Tante, I—I didn't mean to fall in love with him. And I can't go on deceiving him. I know that.' She lifted her chin. 'Tomorrow. I'll try and tell him then.'

'After, one presumes, you have at last rewarded his admirable restraint?' *Madame's* tone of voice conveyed a hint of true Gallic cynicism. 'You are wise, Alys. A well-satisfied man is likely to be more—indulgent.'

Allie's face burned. 'You make me sound so calculating.'

'I think you should be,' her great-aunt said frankly. 'It is time, *ma chère*, that you began to consider, very carefully, your future, and what part in it, if any, is destined for your young doctor. Because,' she added, 'he will undoubtedly wish to know.'

The weather began to change not long after Tante's departure the following morning. Clouds were massing in the west, and the wind had freshened sharply. When Allie, suddenly restless in the confines of Les Sables, went out for a walk, she could hear the roar of the waves, thrashing at the cliffs, and found she was struggling to keep her balance against some of the gusts.

By the time Remy arrived it had begun to rain, and Allie was outside struggling to deal with a recalcitrant shutter.

'Let me do it.' He pushed the stiff bolt into place. '*Madame* is not here?'

'She's spending the day with some people in Vannes.' Allie stood back, dusting her hands. She looked up at the sullen sky, with its scudding dark clouds, and sighed. 'It's hardly a day for the beach.'

'But good, perhaps, for sightseeing.' He kissed her, his mouth warm and lingering on hers, and she felt the pleasure of it lance like wildfire through her body.

She said breathlessly, 'Under cover, I hope?'

'*Naturellement.*'

She collected her bag, and threw a cotton jacket over her black vest top and cream denim skirt.

They had been travelling for several minutes before she realised they were heading towards Trehel.

'But I don't understand,' she began. 'You said—'

'That I had somewhere you would want to see.' He sent her a swift smile. 'And so I have. I hope you will not be disappointed.'

She gasped. 'Your house!' she exclaimed. 'You mean it's actually—finished?'

'All except the work I plan to do myself.' Remy nodded. He added softly, 'And you, *ma belle*, will be my first visitor.'

'Oh.' She felt her face warm. 'Well, I'm—honoured.'

'No.' His voice was gentle. 'The honour, *mon amour*, will be all mine, believe me.'

He was telling her that the waiting was over, and her throat tightened at the promise in his words—just as her body began to tingle in excitement, mingled, at the same time, with a kind of trepidation.

Because Remy might be the one to be disappointed, she thought with a pang of unease. After all, what did she know about pleasing a man? Less than nothing, as she'd been told so many times in the past. And, however much she might love Remy, she was still the same person at heart, and even his patience could not last for ever.

*Frigid—fumbling—useless.* The words were like scars on her psyche.

I don't have to do this, she told herself, swallowing. I can find some excuse. Tell him it's the wrong time of the month. Anything.

Maybe that I've—simply—changed my mind.

Except, of course, he would only have to touch me, she thought, feeling her entire being shiver in anticipation—and yearning...

And then they were at Trehel, and somehow it was too late to turn back, even if she'd wanted to.

It was raining heavily, so Remy parked the Jeep close to the barn, then took her hand and ran with her, pushing open the big double doors.

The room she found herself in was enormous, with a flagged floor, a large stone fireplace at one end, and a state-of-the-art kitchen at the other. Apart from that, it was still completely unfurnished, but Allie could imagine how it would look, with sofas grouped round the fire, and maybe a huge dining table where friends would eat and talk late into the evening.

But the really breathtaking feature was the long range of arched full-length windows opposite the entrance, with panoramic views over the paddock and the wooded hills beyond it.

Even with rain sweeping across in great swathes, the outlook was spectacular.

She said, with a catch in her voice, 'It's—amazing.' She wandered into the kitchen, running her hand along the marble work surfaces, admiring the gleaming oven and hob with lifted brows. 'Does it all work?'

'But of course.' Remy mimed mock pique. 'Shall I prove it by making you some coffee?' He paused. 'Or would you prefer to see the rest of the house?'

'The rest—I think.' She felt suddenly shy, her heart

pounding as they walked towards the wooden staircase that led to the upper floor.

Say something, she adjured herself. Try to sound casual. Normal.

'Do you know yet how you're going to furnish it?'

Oh, God, she sounded as if she was presenting a makeover programme on television.

'I have already begun.' At the top of the stairs, Remy opened a door, and stood back to let her precede him into what was clearly the master bedroom. It was another big room, soaring up into the barn's original vaulted roof, with windows on two sides capturing every atom of light, and its expanse of wooden floor softened with sheepskin rugs.

But, above all, there was the wide bed, made even more massive by its high, ornately carved headboard. Dominating the entire space as it was clearly intended to do.

And, she realised, freshly made up, too, with crisp white linen and a glamorous satin coverlet the colour of sapphires. Mounded with snowy pillows. Waiting…

She halted, eyes widening, as she began to tremble, and felt his arms go round her, drawing her back against him. Holding her strongly.

He said quietly, 'Lie with me, Alys. Lie with me here, in my house. In my bed.'

And she turned, lifting her face for his kiss and whispering, 'Yes,' against the warm urgency of his mouth.

# CHAPTER SEVEN

His kiss was deep and yearning, as if he was seeking her soul through her lips, and Allie sank against him as a strange weakness invaded her body, her eyes closing and her hands clinging to his shoulders.

He raised his head at last, framing her face in his hands, looking down at her, gravely and searchingly.

'You are shaking, *mon amour*,' he told her quietly. 'In truth, am I so terrifying?'

'No—oh, no.' The denial tumbled from her. 'Oh, Remy, I'm such a fool, but I couldn't bear it if you were—disappointed in me.'

He put a silencing finger on her lips. 'I love you, Alys. And that is all that matters.' His voice was very gentle. 'Pleasing each other with our bodies is a joy we shall learn together.'

He slipped her damp jacket from her shoulders and let it drop, then lifted her into his arms and carried her across the room to the bed, throwing back the sapphire quilt before placing her with great care against the heaped pillows. Then, kicking off his shoes, he came to lie beside her.

She turned on her side to face him, her hand going shyly to brush a strand of thick dark hair back from his forehead, and he captured her fingers, brushing them softly with his mouth.

'You are the dream of my life, Alys,' he murmured, then began to kiss her, his lips touching her forehead, her eyes, her cheekbones and her pliant mouth in a series of brief, delicate caresses that seemed to give but then withdraw. Which tantalised but offered no immediate satisfaction.

Yet that was what she wanted, she realised, startled. What she'd craved ever since that first afternoon at Les Sables, when she'd first felt the touch of his hands on her bare skin.

She longed to be taken—to feel him inside her and know the heated steel of his arousal as he possessed her.

She moved closer, pressing herself against him, her lips finding the opening of his shirt, pushing the crisp cotton aside to caress the base of his throat before moving down to the warm hair-roughened skin of his chest.

Remy groaned softly. *'Doucement, mon ange,'* he ordered, his voice faintly breathless. 'I want to make this good for you, and for that I shall need every atom of control I possess.'

She looked up at him, running the tip of her tongue slowly round her lips. 'Are you—really so sure of that, *monsieur*?'

'Ask me again, *chérie*—later,' he told her huskily, and recaptured her mouth with his.

His hand moved to her breast and stroked it gently, moulding its softness and cupping it in his palm, before allowing his fingers to trace her nipple with a delicate precision that made her gasp as he brought it to sharply delineated arousal against the clinging material of her top.

For a moment he looked down at her, surveying the exquisite havoc he had created, the vivid eyes darkening.

'You are wearing too many clothes, *mon amour*.' His voice was a whisper.

He slipped down the straps of her top, freeing her arms, then deftly tugged the little garment over her head and tossed it aside, baring her to the waist. For a brief, searing moment she was acutely aware of her body—almost ashamed of how slender it was—how slight the curves he'd just uncovered. And her hands went up to conceal them.

But he guessed her intention and blocked her, his fingers closing firmly round her wrists.

'Don't hide, Alys,' he murmured. 'Not when I have waited so long to see you like this. Show me, *ma belle*, how truly lovely you are.'

He bent his head, his mouth slowly adoring each swollen rosy peak in turn, the erotic brush of his tongue creating a new, aching excitement that was echoed deep inside. She sighed, her hips moving restlessly, as the sweet, languorous torment continued, her nipples throbbing with a pleasure that was almost akin to pain.

When he raised his head at last, she lay looking up at him, her eyes dazed, her ragged breath sobbing in her throat.

His hands stroked their way down her body to the waistband of her skirt. He undid the small metal button at the front, then the short zip, easing the fabric gently over her hips until she was completely free of it and it could also be discarded.

Leaving her with just the minimal modesty of a pair of tiny lace briefs.

Remy made a small sound in his throat, then gathered her to him so closely that his clothing grazed her skin, his mouth closing on hers in a new and fierce demand.

She responded almost wildly, her lips parting eagerly to receive the thrust of his tongue, her hands tangling in the thick dark hair to hold him to her.

And then his mouth began to move slowly downwards, caressing her throat, her shoulders, and the little valley between her breasts, while all the time his hands were stroking her with sensuous delight, lingering in the hollow of her hip, drifting across the faint concavity of her belly, seeking out the silken length of her thighs.

Touching, at last, the lace that was her only covering. Pushing it aside so that his fingers could reach the slick core of her. Moving on her gently, but with such exquisite precision that when he paused she moaned aloud, her body rearing against him.

'*Oui, mon amour.*' His voice was raw with hunger. 'Yes—and yes.'

And then, at last, the lace too was gone, peeled deftly away, and she was naked in his arms, with no barrier left to his skilfully questing hands.

Or—dear God—his mouth…

For a moment, shock held her frozen. Then, 'No—please—you can't…' Her voice was a small, shaken whimper of distress. She tried to push his head away from her slackened thighs, but Remy's hands were closing round her wrists, anchoring them effortlessly to the bed so that this new invasion of her most intimate self could continue entirely unhampered.

And her desperate attempts to evade his caress were only making matters a thousand times worse.

With devastating purpose, his lips sought the hot moist petals of her womanhood, parting them so that his tongue could search out the tiny hidden bud within and tease it into delicious tumescent arousal.

And at each sensuous stroke she felt her writhing body succumbing to a languorous weakness, her physical consciousness shifting—spiralling helplessly to a plane whose existence she'd never guessed at before.

Until, at last, there came a moment when she no longer wanted to escape what he was doing to her, even if it had ever been possible.

She heard her breathing change, and the spiral of feeling became an irresistible force, carrying her upwards to some unknown peak of desire. A moan of agonised pleasure burst from her throat, and her body arched rapturously in sheer surrender to wave after wave of utterly voluptuous delight.

And as the storm subsided she lay panting, her sated body damp with sweat, aware that there were tears on her face. She tried to wipe them away with trembling hands, and Remy gathered her in his arms, whispering softly to her in his own language, words of reassurance, words of love, telling her how sweet she was, how clever and how beautiful, while she clung to him, her mouth quivering into a smile.

And when he eventually released her it was only so that he could more easily strip off his own clothing. Allie lay watching him through half-closed eyes as he swiftly undressed, her body shivering in renewed and unforeseen hunger when he turned back to her, naked and magnificently aroused.

It seemed impossible that her body could be capable of such desire so soon again, she thought as she opened her arms to him eagerly, taking him into her embrace and running her hands over his shoulders and back, glorying in the strength of bone and muscle—the texture of his skin. And yet she was burning up for him—melting with need.

'Do I please you, *ma belle*?' There was a smile in the huskiness of his voice as he lifted himself over her—above her. For answer, she clasped her fingers round his jutting hardness, letting her hand slowly travel its length in an appreciation that was as teasing as it was overt.

'*Sorcière*,' he whispered hoarsely. 'Witch.' And he took her with one deep, lingering thrust. She cried out in bewildered joy at the potency—the completeness of their union as he filled her. Knowing that here, at last, was the ultimate in consummation.

For a moment, he paused. 'There is no problem?'

'None.' He was so anxious for her, but it wasn't necessary. Surely he could tell how much she wanted him? she thought, half-dizzy with this new sensation, her inner muscles clenching round him—holding him.

Remy began to move without haste, his lean hips driving powerfully as he carried her with him into the surging ebb and flow of passion, and she responded avidly, instinctively, matching the rhythmic motion he was creating, her hands digging into his shoulders as her legs lifted to enclose him. To lock round him.

At once she sensed a new urgency in him that he was clearly struggling to restrain, and she knew that he was still trying to be patient, to wait until she was ready to accompany him to their mutual release.

But I, she thought, want it now...

She smiled into his eyes, her lashes sweeping down onto desire-flushed cheeks, letting her hands follow a leisurely path down his back to the flat male buttocks and stroking them with her palms, while one finger traced a delicate, enticing pattern on the sensitive nerve-endings at the base of his spine.

She heard his involuntary gasp, felt the pace of his possession quicken suddenly—fiercely. Recognised with candid female triumph the almost remorseless increase in its intensity that she had coaxed from him.

Was aware of a stirring deep inside her in reply, as warm tendrils of sensation began to spread, to intensify in their turn, splintering what little was left of her control.

Then, a voice she hardly recognised as hers cried out in wild disbelief, as the frenzy of her senses sent her pulsating body into soaring and ecstatic climax.

And Remy followed her, her name wrenched with a groan from his straining throat as he reached the frantic culmination of his own pleasure, and she felt his exhausted weight slump across her, his head heavy on her breasts as he tried to calm the tortured rasp of his breathing.

And she was content to lie like that, holding him tightly, her lips caressing the strands of sweat-dampened hair on his forehead.

Because instinct seemed to be telling her that if ever there was a moment for confession, this was it. When he was in her arms, his sated, emptied body still joined to hers like this, surely he would forgive her anything—wouldn't he?

'Remy.' His name was a breath from her lips. She put her cheek on his hair. 'Darling—there's something I have to say. Something I should have told you long ago—when we first met. Only I never knew—never guessed—we would love each other. That you would mean everything in the world to me.'

She swallowed. 'Sweetheart—*mon amour*... I— I'm married. I have a husband in England. But I don't love him, and I never did. So I'm going back to finish it, get a divorce.'

She ended on a little rush of words, and waited tautly for his response. Only there was none.

She was prepared for shock—certainly for anger and recriminations—but not—silence.

Or was he simply too stunned to speak?

She said questioningly, 'Remy—darling…?'

He mumbled something drowsy in reply, burying his face more closely against her, his body totally relaxed, his breathing deep and steady.

My God, she thought with an inward groan, he's asleep. Which means he hasn't heard a single word I've said, even though it took every atom of courage I possess to say it.

She was tempted to wake him there and then—to repeat her stumbling confession. But he looked altogether too peaceful, all tension gone from the dark face. He was even smiling a little as he slept.

Well, Allie thought, sighing. I suppose it will keep a little longer at that. But I must tell him soon—very soon. And, on that resolve, she closed her own eyes and allowed herself to drift slowly away.

She awoke with a start, and lay for a moment totally disorientated, her heart thudding. Hugo, she thought. Oh, God, I was dreaming about Hugo.

Then she heard the rain still lashing the window and realised where she was, and why, and relief and joy flooded through her.

She turned her head slowly and looked at Remy, still fast asleep beside her. At some point he must have moved a little, lifted himself away from her, although his arm was still thrown possessively across her waist.

Did he know? she wondered with passionate tenderness. Did he have the least idea how she was feeling? Did he understand her starved body's reaction to the miracle of physical delight he'd created for her?

For the first time in years she felt totally relaxed and at peace. Also happier than she had ever believed possible.

And when he woke she would tell him so, along with, she decided, a suitable reviver.

She slid carefully from under the protection of his arm and swung her feet to the floor. From the tangle of clothing beside the bed she retrieved Remy's shirt and slipped it on, fastening a few discreet buttons on the way. She could detect the faint fragrance of the cologne he used, and she put the sleeve to her nose, sniffing luxuriously.

She pulled the coverlet over him, then padded quietly out of the room and downstairs to the kitchen, where she stood looking around her, getting her bearings.

He'd offered her coffee some lifetime ago, she told herself, so the makings had to be available.

She looked first in the refrigerator, finding milk, and mineral water too, and she uncapped one of the small bottles, drinking thirstily as she leant back against the work surface.

This would be an amazing kitchen to work in, she thought, imagining herself here with Remy, preparing a meal together.

She sighed, smiling. Well—perhaps—one of these days. But coffee would do to be going on with.

Inspection of the pale wood cupboards eventually yielded a pack of ground beans and a *cafetière*, so she filled the elegant stainless steel kettle and set it to boil, humming quietly to herself as she did so. She'd just located a set of earthenware beakers when she heard a sound behind her and turned quickly.

Solange was standing in the middle of the living room, staring at her, lips parted, eyes burning with anger and disbelief in her white face.

And Allie knew, of course, what the other girl must be seeing. The dishevelled hair, the half-buttoned shirt reaching only to mid-thigh, the shining eyes and swollen mouth. Everything about her, she realised with dismay, must be screaming Sex.

Oh, God, she thought. Why didn't I get dressed properly?

'*Chienne.*' Solange's voice shook. '*Sale vache.*'

For a moment, all Allie wanted to do was run. To get away from the fury and the ugly words. And from the French girl's bitter disappointment, too—which, perhaps, was the worst thing of all. But she stood her ground, lifting her chin defiantly.

'Please don't call me names, *mademoiselle*,' she said quietly. 'I am neither a bitch nor a dirty cow. I have been making love with the man I love, and I have nothing to be ashamed of.'

Solange took a step closer, her hands balled into fists at her sides. 'You don't think so? But I tell you

different. Because you do not belong here, you—
*espèce de raclure*.' Her tone was a hiss. 'You are an
outsider—not one of us—and Remy needs a woman
beside him who can support him in his work.
Someone who knows this community—who has its
respect. Not a slut of an English girl who will soon be
gone, back to her own filthy country.'

Allie was almost reeling under this onslaught, but
she made herself stay ice-calm. And her voice reflected this. 'I think Remy is free to make his own
choices, Mademoiselle Geran.'

'And what is this great choice? To degrade himself
with a *putaine* like you? Well, he will soon regret that.'
The other woman drew a deep, shuddering breath.
'Always—always I knew what you were. Knew that
you could not wait to throw yourself into his bed.'

'What exactly are you complaining about?' Allie
asked coldly. 'That I have taken your place—or that
you never received an invitation?'

Solange gasped, and her head went back as if Allie
had struck her, the once pretty face twisted with rage
and crimson with mottled blood. She lifted her hands,
bunched into a semblance of claws, and her voice was
thick. 'Would he still want you, I wonder, if I
scratched out your eyes?'

From the stairs, Remy said grimly, 'An interesting
point, Solange, but we will not put it to the test. And
now I think you should go, before you make matters
any worse.'

His feet were bare, concealing his approach, and

he'd clearly dragged on his jeans simply for the sake of marginal decency, because they hung, only half-fastened, low on his hips.

Solange's small red-tipped hands were suddenly uncurled. Extended in appeal.

'Remy, *chéri*, I do not blame you for this. A man has—temptations.' She tried, horribly, to laugh. 'I—I understand this, and I can forgive—'

But he cut coldly across the stumbling words. 'There is no need for forgiveness, Solange. Let me speak plainly. Local gossip may have paired us together, yet I have asked nothing from you, and promised nothing in return. This—understanding between us does not exist.'

She swallowed harshly. 'Remy—*mon coeur*—how can you say that?'

'Because it is true, and you know it.' He paused. 'And I would prefer you did not visit here again without an invitation.'

She stared at him wild-eyed, her mouth working soundlessly, then she whirled round and was gone, the big doors slamming behind her.

Remy leapt the last few stairs and came to Allie's side, sliding his arms round her and drawing her protectively against him. She buried her face in his bare brown shoulder, her voice muffled. 'That was—vile.'

'I woke up and you were gone, which troubled me.' His voice was uneven. 'And then I heard talking, and thought that my father might have arrived, or Grandpapa, and that this could cause you embarrassment.'

'I came down to make coffee,' she said. 'And she was suddenly—here. But why?'

'It is entirely my fault,' Remy said harshly. 'She used to visit often, while the work was being done, in order to find fault with Gaston Levecq, and, I think, to persuade me to employ her cousin instead. Also to offer advice that I did not need. I should have realised—and stopped it when it first began.'

The kettle came cheerfully to the boil and switched itself off. Remy released her and went to fill the *cafetière*.

He said quietly, not looking at her, 'Alys, tell me, *je t'en prie*, that she has not made you hate this house—or regret what has happened between us here.'

'No.' She shook her head vehemently. 'No one— not even Solange—could ever do that.'

She saw the tension relax from his shoulders. He said softly, *'Soit.'* And continued making the coffee.

He said, over his shoulder, 'I am relieved that it was not Grandpapa who found you just now. Seeing you like that might have provoked *une petite crise cardiaque.'*

'At least I'm wearing something,' Allie returned with mock defensiveness. 'And your shirt was the first thing I found on the floor,' she added, not altogether truthfully.

*'Vraiment?'* The brilliant eyes were dancing with amusement. 'Perhaps I should make you a present of it, *chérie*. I know it never looked so good on me.'

She said huskily, 'Everything looks good on you, Remy.' Adding silently, *And off, too…*

'*Ma bien-aimée.*' His voice was gentle. He was silent for a moment. 'It was a bad moment for me, when I found you gone from our bed. I thought perhaps you were angry with me.'

'Angry?' She was startled. 'How could I be?'

His mouth twisted ruefully. 'Then—disappointed. Because I wished to make it perfect for you—our first time together—to take away all the bad memories. But it was over far too soon.' He added with a faint groan, 'And then I fell asleep.' He shook his head. 'My only excuse, *mon ange*, is that I wanted you so very much.'

She went to him, sliding her arms round his waist and smiling up into his eyes. 'That sounds more like a very good reason than an excuse,' she told him softly, and stood on tiptoe to kiss his mouth. She added teasingly, 'And may I remind you that we both went to sleep?'

She wanted to assure him, too, that the bad memories were all gone. But how could she when there was still the appalling problem of her marriage to be dealt with? she thought, conscious of a nervous tightening in the pit of her stomach. She pressed herself more closely against him, letting the warmth of his body dispel the sudden chill inside her.

He put a finger under her chin, tilting her face up towards him. 'Yet there is something, I think, that troubles you.'

She forced a smile. 'The aftermath of Solange, I expect. She did call me some pretty foul names.'

There was a pause, then he said laconically, '*D'accord*. That must be it.'

I can fix everything, Allie told herself fiercely, as she drank the coffee he'd poured for her. Somehow, I'll make Hugo see that it was all a terrible mistake, which needs to be put right. After all, he's had time to think too. He must know that it can't go on. All it needs is a little goodwill on both sides.

She was sharply aware that Remy was watching her thoughtfully, and lowered her lashes with deliberate demureness. 'Has no one told you, *monsieur*, that it's rude to stare?'

'It would be a greater insult to ignore you, *ma belle*.' His tone was dry. 'And I stare for a purpose, you understand.'

'Which is?' She replaced the empty beaker on the counter top.

'I am making a picture of you in my head, Alys, to carry with me always.'

'Dressed like this?' Laughing, she posed, hand on hip.

'*Pourquoi pas?* But with a little adjustment, perhaps.' He leaned across and undid two more buttons on the shirt, then gently pushed it from her shoulder, exposing one pink-tipped breast. 'Mmm,' he murmured in soft appreciation. '*Perfection*. If we have to be apart, I have only to remember how you look at this moment.'

Ludicrous to feel shy after the intimacies they'd shared, but her skin warmed just the same.

'And what about me?' she challenged with a touch of breathlessness. 'May I have a picture to remember too?'

She reached for the zip on his jeans, but he captured her hands, laughing. 'You may have any image you desire, *mon amour*—but in the bedroom, perhaps, in case more unwanted visitors arrive.'

He kissed her, his mouth hot and fierce on hers, and she laughed back and ran with him, aglow and willing, towards the stairs, and the waiting bed.


A long time later, she said drowsily, 'I must go. Tante Madelon will be back by now, and wondering where I am.'

Remy trailed a lazy hand the length of her body. 'I think she will know, *chérie*, don't you?'

She moved pleasurably against the ingenious questing of his fingers. 'Almost certainly, darling. But we don't need to underline the fact.'

He rolled over suddenly, imprisoning her under his body. 'I don't want to let you go,' he told her huskily. 'I need you to stay here with me, *mon coeur*. To sleep in my arms tonight.'

'How can I?' Allie appealed ruefully. 'Tante is obviously trying to be understanding, but she has her limits, especially as I'm her guest.' She paused. 'Besides, she'll certainly expect us to be discreet.'

Remy sighed. '*Tu as raison, ma mie.* I am not thinking as I should—perhaps because I feel I am almost scared to let you out of my sight.'

She put up a hand, her fingers tender against the roughness of his chin, her voice teasing. 'Haven't you had enough of me, *monsieur*?'

He said quietly, 'I have been waiting for you my whole life, Alys. I shall never have enough.' He slid his hands under her flanks, raising her a little, so that, slowly and sweetly, he could enter once more her rapturously acceptant body.

Unlike the fierce, searing passion they'd shared earlier, when he'd taken her to some blind, mindless sphere where she'd thought she might die, this time it was a gentle almost meditative union, composed of sighs and murmurs, and subtle, exquisite pressures, so that the moment of climax rippled through her like a soft breeze across a lake. And her voice broke as she whispered his name.

Afterwards, Allie lay supine, her eyes closed, her body languid with fulfillment. But as she felt him leaving the bed, she lifted herself on to an elbow. 'Where are you going?'

'To take you back to Les Sables—after I have taken a shower.'

She smiled mischievously up at him. 'You don't want company?'

He gave her a wry look. '*Oui, naturellement.* But I am trying to learn to do without you, *ma mie.*'

She tutted reprovingly as she swung her legs to the floor and followed him into the bathroom. 'That sounds like a very dull lesson. Now, I think, my darling, that you should make the most of me when I'm around,' she added serenely as she joined him in the glass cubicle under the power spray. She poured some shower gel into her hands and began to lather his body, beginning with his shoulders, then moving downwards across his chest to his abdomen, and lower, her fingers working in small, enticing circles. 'Don't you agree?'

'*Dieu,*' he said hoarsely. 'You are insatiable. You will kill me.'

She glanced down, and laughed softly. 'Even though the evidence suggests otherwise, my love?'

'But will the evidence be strong enough to prove your case, *mon ange*?' He turned the shower full on, then reached for her, lifting her off the tiled floor, and locking her legs round his hips. '*Eh bien,* there is only one way to find out.'

She said tremulously, 'Remy—oh, God—Remy…'

It was twilight when they eventually arrived at Les Sables, but there was no light in the house, and Tante's car was missing from its usual parking place.

'I seem to have beaten her to it,' Allie said, as she opened the door. 'Perhaps I can convince her that I spent the day here quietly on my own.'

'I doubt it.' Remy followed her in. '*Madame* is a woman who has loved. She will recognise the signs.'

'And you,' she said, 'are altogether too pleased with yourself.'

He slid a hand under the fall of still-damp hair, and kissed the nape of her neck. 'But I am pleased with you, also, *chérie*. Does that excuse me?'

The sound of the telephone made them both jump.

'Is that Madame de Marchington—the great-niece of Madame Colville?' an elderly-sounding male voice enquired when Allie picked up the receiver. 'Ah, *bon*.

I am Emil Blanchard. I regret to tell you that Madelon slipped on the wet pavement outside our house as she was leaving her car, and fell.'

'She fell?' Allie echoed, dismayed. 'Oh, God, is she badly hurt?'

'No, no. Our doctor made a thorough examination. But she is shocked, and bruised, of course, and it would not be wise for her to drive. So we have persuaded her to remain with us for a few days until she has recovered.' He added with faint peevishness, 'I have attempted to telephone you several times before, *madame*, but could get no answer.'

'No, I've also been out—visiting friends. I'm sorry.' Allie hesitated. 'Thank you for telling me, and please give Tante Madelon my love. I hope she's fine—very soon—and tell her that I'll take good care of the house.'

*'Pauvre madame,'* Remy said soberly, when Allie outlined exactly what had happened. 'Such accidents can be serious at her age, but fortunately she seems to have escaped lasting damage.' He paused, his expression quizzical. 'But this means, *ma belle,* that you will be alone in this isolated place. Will you feel safe?'

'Oh, I'm sure I'll be fine during the day,' Allie assured him. She also paused. 'But I might be nervous at night,' she added pensively.

'If you have problems with your nerves, *ma belle,*' Remy said solemnly, 'then you should always call a doctor.'

She said softly, 'I think I just did.' And walked happily into his arms.

# CHAPTER EIGHT

ALLIE came back to the present with a start, to the realisation that she was shivering violently. The night air had gone from cool to cold now, and the last thing she needed was pneumonia, she thought, her mouth twisting wryly as she closed the back door and locked it.

Or maybe the last thing she really wanted was to go upstairs and try to sleep in that room—in the bed she'd once shared with Remy.

She'd known from the first that that was, inevitably, where she'd be expected to spend her nights, but up to now she hadn't allowed herself to think about that too closely, or examine how she would feel when she had to lie there alone.

When she would not feel the warmth of Remy's arms, the murmur of his voice, or the beloved weight of him as, stunned and breathless, they lay wrapped together after climax. Or even the steady rhythm of his heartbeat under her cheek as she drifted blissfully to sleep.

For a moment she leaned forward, leaning her forehead against the stout panels of the door as the pain of it lanced through her.

Oh, God, she thought. Knowing the truth as I did, how could I have allowed myself to be so happy? To keep silent, even though I was virtually living with him? When I was breathing and dreaming him through every passing hour?

She drew a deep breath, composing herself, then switched off the lights and made her way slowly upstairs.

Tom was sleeping peacefully, and did not stir as she trod over to the cot to check on him. She sank down on the rug beside him, her back to the wall, her arms clasping her knees in the darkness.

Moonlight had filled the room each time she'd slept there with Remy, she thought wistfully. The majority of their nights, however, had been spent at Trehel, because Remy had been concerned that Tante might regard his presence at Les Sables as an intrusion, and hadn't wanted to risk the older woman's disapproval.

The new house had occupied their time, too, when his work was done, as she'd helped him begin to turn its empty spaces into a home. Two massive sofas in pale leather had been delivered, and a hunt round the local antiques outlets had produced a substantial table and six elegant chairs.

He'd taken her shopping at the morning markets, and she had revelled in the fresh vegetables and the endless varieties of seafood on offer. Oysters were one of Remy's passions, and he'd taught her to open them with a special knife, then eat them with a squeeze of lemon juice and a sprinkle of pepper.

Mealtimes had become a delicious adventure, from

the preparation stage and the cooking, down to the last crumb of cheese.

Allie had bloomed under his tutelage, and she'd known it, as her life opened up in all kinds of ways. She had even learned to ride, with the surprisingly patient Roland enduring endless circuits of the paddock on a leading rein.

And she'd soon found that Remy's work could affect him profoundly—as when he'd come back to Trehel, grey-faced and numb, having lost a five-year-old whose parents had not recognised the symptoms to viral meningitis, after an all-night battle at the local hospital. She had learned, too, that at such times he would turn to her body for his own healing, letting their mutual passion assuage in some way his anger and sense of failure.

Tante had remained in Vannes with her friends. She'd explained that she had twisted her ankle in the fall, and that the swelling was taking longer than expected to go down, but Allie had wondered wryly if her absence was prompted more by tact than actual infirmity, and if her great-aunt was hoping their attraction to each other would have burned itself out by the time she returned.

She'd spoken to Tante on the phone every day, but by tacit agreement there had been no reference between them to her relationship with Remy, or the increasingly vexed question of her marital status and its resolution.

With each day that had passed, the right moment

for such a confession had seemed to became more and more difficult to find. And the longer she'd left it, the worse it had become.

She'd begun to feel as if her happiness with Remy was the equivalent of holding thistledown cupped in her hand, knowing that one strong blast of reality could destroy it for ever.

On the plus side, Solange, since the afternoon when she'd slammed out of the house, had kept her distance, although once or twice in Ignac Allie had gained the impression that she was being watched, and with no friendly eye either. But she'd spotted nothing, so maybe, she'd told herself, she was just being paranoid.

Yet the vague feeling of unease had persisted, as if she'd sensed that somewhere a thunderstorm was hovering that would bring the bright golden days of sunshine to an end.

And I was right, Allie thought, wearily raking a hand through her hair and staring ahead of her with eyes that saw nothing. Ah, dear God, I was so right…

The day had begun calmly enough, she recalled. It had been a Saturday, and Remy had had no surgery, so, after visiting the market, they'd driven to Carnac and spent the morning on the beach there, quitting the sands when they'd begun to get crowded in order to enjoy a late and leisurely lunch.

'I'd better go to Les Sables,' Allie mused as they drove back. 'I haven't set foot there for two days, and it might have burned down.'

Remy raised an eyebrow. 'I think word might have reached us by now, *ma chère*,' he drawled.

She sighed. 'I know, but I'd still better check it out. Besides, I need some more clothes.'

'*D'accord.*' As he pulled up outside the house, his arm went round her shoulders, scooping her close, his lips meeting hers in a frankly sensuous caress. 'I shall see you later, then, at Trehel,' he told her, adding huskily, 'And don't keep me waiting too long, *chérie*, because tonight is going to be a very special meal.'

Her heartbeat jolted a little in sudden excitement, mixed with a touch of panic as her instinct warned her where the evening might lead.

Swallowing, she touched his cheek. 'I won't be late.'

She paused at the door to wave, and saw his hand lift in a smiling salute as he drove away.

So the moment had come, she thought, as she turned slowly and went indoors. Remy planned to talk about their future together. She knew it. Therefore she could afford no more evasion—no more prevarication.

And she would have to speak first. Lay all her cards on the table. Explain to him that she'd dreaded saying anything that could detract from their happiness in each other, and ask for his understanding.

The first real test for both of us, she thought wryly. But if he really loves me…

She shook herself out of her reverie. Her best course was to get over to Trehel as quickly as possible and tell him everything. And, as he'd made it clear this was going to be an occasion, she would dress for that too.

Soften his justifiable wrath by making herself look as enticing as possible—by appealing directly to his senses. And she knew how.

There was a dress that he'd never seen, a black silky slip of a thing, with narrow straps and a neckline that dipped far more daringly than usual, making it discreetly obvious that it required only the minimum of underclothing. She'd put it into her case on sheer impulse, but she realised now there would never be a better time to wear it.

She went up to her room, stripping off shorts and tee-shirt, and the bikini she was wearing beneath them, then showered, shampooing her hair at the same time, to get rid of all traces of salt and sand.

She might wear it up for a change, she thought, smiling to herself as she imagined Remy unfastening the clip at some point, and letting the soft strands spill through his fingers.

She applied her favourite scented body lotion, then drew on a pair of tiny black lace briefs. For a long moment she looked at herself in the full-length mirror, assessing almost clinically the seductive effect of the little black triangle against the creaminess of her skin.

I'm not a beauty, she thought, but please—*please*—let him find me beautiful tonight. Let him desire me so much that nothing else matters. That, in spite of everything, he'll know that he can't live without me—and he'll forgive me what I have to say, and wait until I'm free to come to him. *Oh, please…*

She zipped herself into the dress, then picked up a

comb and began experimenting with her hair. She paused, her attention arrested by the sound of a vehicle approaching fast.

It sounds like the Jeep, she thought, bewildered, and one swift glance from the window confirmed this.

He's come to fetch me, she thought ruefully, and I'm not nearly ready yet.

Still barefoot, she began to descend the stairs, halting, a smile playing round her lips, as the door was flung wide and Remy strode into the living room below.

'You're impatient, *monsieur*,' she teased. 'You've spoiled my surprise.'

Then she saw his face and gasped, her hand tightening convulsively on the stair-rail.

He was as white as a sheet, his skin drawn tautly across his cheekbones, his mouth harshly compressed. The vivid eyes stared up at her, the ice of their contempt searing her like a living flame, and she realised he was holding something like a sheaf of papers, rolled in his hand.

'A surprise, *madame*?' His voice cut like a knife. 'I think I have been surprised enough for one day.'

He tossed the papers he was holding towards the foot of the stairs, and she realised they were, in fact, the pages of a glossy magazine.

She said hoarsely, 'I—I don't understand.'

'Then you have a short memory, *madame*,' Remy returned with paralysing scorn. 'Also a selective one, if you have managed to so conveniently forget your own wedding.'

And then, at last, Allie remembered. Oh, God, she thought with a kind of sick despair, that dreadful interview with *County* magazine that Grace had insisted on—the ghastly pictures they took of me in my dress and veil, posing me beside Hugo so it wouldn't be quite as obvious that he was in a wheelchair. The whole appalling farce. How could I ever have forgotten? Yet I did. And now—*now*—it's come back to haunt me.

She looked down at the crumpled magazine. Forced frozen lips to ask, 'Where did you find it?'

'I did not,' he denied curtly. 'Solange Geran was throwing away some old magazines her English guests had left in one of the *gîtes*, and she saw the photograph. Read the story of the bride and groom whose love triumphed over adversity.' His laugh was corrosive in its bitterness. 'A romantic story she could not wait to share with me, *naturellement*.'

Solange, she thought with a terrible weariness. Of course...

She bent her head. 'Remy—I can explain...'

'But how? By telling me that you have an identical twin who happens to share your given name? Or some other lie to add to the rest?'

The savagery in his voice made her shrink. If she hadn't been gripping the rail, she would probably have fallen.

Instead, she forced herself to stand her ground, struggling to control her voice—to hide the hideous debilitating weakness that was making her tremble all over. Because somehow she had to make him listen to her. Salvage something out of the wreckage of her hopes and dreams.

'No, it's true,' she said with quiet weariness. 'I—I am married.' She lifted her chin. 'But I was going to tell you. I—I swear it.'

'Ah, but when, *madame*?' Remy asked with cruel mockery. 'Did you plan to wait for our wedding night, perhaps? Inform me then that I had become a bigamist?'

Her throat tightened to an agony. Tears glittered on her lashes. 'Remy—don't—please.'

'Why should I spare you? he flung at her. 'When from the first you have lied to me—deceived me in this vile way?'

'I—I wanted to tell you. I—did try…'

He said slowly, 'If you had worn your ring and used your married name, then I would have known from the first. I would never have approached you.' He shook his head. 'But you did not. And Madame Colville encouraged you in this. *C'est incroyable.*'

'No,' she said. 'You mustn't blame Tante Madelon. She did her best to persuade me—to do the right thing. If I didn't, then it's my fault alone.'

'Yes.' His tone was starkly accusing. 'You—alone, as I now see.' He threw his head back, staring up at her with eyes as cold and remote as a polar ocean. *'Mon Dieu*, Alys, you knew that I loved you, and you—you let me think that you loved me in turn.'

'I did,' she said. 'I *do*. Darling, you must believe that—'

'You have a strange idea of love, *madame*. Presumably you loved your husband when you married him. Yet within only a few months of your marriage you broke your vows and gave yourself to me. The date of your wedding is given—here.' He walked across to the foot of the stairs and kicked the magazine. 'Isn't it a little early for such flagrant infidelity? What kind of a woman does such a thing?'

*A desperate one...*

She winced inwardly. 'I never meant you to find out—like this.'

His mouth curled. 'Now, that I do believe.'

'And I didn't marry for love,' she went on desperately. 'If you read the text with the photograph, you'll know that my—that Hugo was very badly injured in a polo accident. He's never been my husband in any real sense.'

'Then why did you marry him?' he asked scathingly. 'For money? For his title? And did you find then that it was not enough? I think maybe it was so.'

His laugh jeered at her. 'And so you came to France— to find yourself a lover and enjoy a little sexual adventure, *n'est-ce pas?* Was that my purpose in your life, *madame*? To ease for you the frustration of a disappointing marriage? I hope I gave satisfaction.'

'No,' she whispered. 'No—please—it wasn't like that. I never expected to meet you—to fall in love,' she added on a little sob.

The dark, bitter face did not soften. 'I never hid my attraction to you, Alys. You knew from the first how it was with me. Yet you never stepped back,' he said harshly. 'Never warned me that legally and morally you were beyond my reach.'

He took a deep breath. 'God knows, I am no saint, but I would never knowingly allow myself to become entangled with another man's wife, any more than I would knock him down in the street and rob him.

'But that is not everything,' he added grimly. 'That day at the standing stones I told you plainly that I needed you to trust me, but in spite of that you still kept your secret hidden—because you could not bring yourself to confide in me. And that, perhaps, is the greatest hurt—the worst betrayal of all.'

'I so wanted to.' Her voice shook. 'But I was—afraid I'd lose you.'

'No trust,' he said, flatly. 'And no faith either. *Ah, Dieu.*'

'I was going to tell you this evening,' she said huskily. 'Darling, I swear it. I had it all planned.'

'But of course,' he returned with cold mockery. 'Was it to have been before or after I committed the ultimate folly of asking you to marry me?'

'Remy, don't say that.' She spoke jerkily. 'I know I've done everything the wrong way, and I blame myself completely. But, please, can't we sit down and talk properly? I need to make you understand—'

'But I understand quite well, *madame.*' He interrupted her stumbling words with swift impatience. 'You have made fools of us both—your husband and your lover. But he at least will never know that you have cheated him so monstrously. So he is the fortunate one.' He gave her one last scornful look. 'Although I do not envy him,' he added, and turned to go.

'Remy.' His name burst pleadingly from her throat. 'Don't do this to me—to both of us. Don't leave like this.'

He halted. Swung back, and walked up the stairs to her, his hand closing on her wrist, not gently.

'Then how, Alys?' There was a note in his voice that jarred her senses. 'Or do you hope, perhaps, for a more intimate *adieu*? For me to pay a final visit to your charmingly eager body?'

He shrugged, his mouth set in a sneer. '*Eh bien, pourquoi pas?* All else may be gone, but sex still remains. What a practical girl you are, *ma belle*.' He swung her off her feet almost negligently, carrying her up the stairs.

For a moment Allie was stunned, then she began to struggle against his bruising grip, pushing against his chest with clenched fists.

'No—Remy—no.' It was a cry of fear as well as anger. 'I didn't mean that. Put me down—now.'

But he ignored her protests, shouldering his way into her bedroom, and when he set her on her feet it was only so that he could access her zip more easily. Halfway down, it stuck, and he took the edges of her dress in strong relentless hands and dragged them apart. She heard the stitching rip irrevocably, then the silky fabric slithered down her body and pooled around her feet, leaving her, she knew, as good as naked under the inimical intensity of his gaze. Then he picked her up again, with almost insulting ease, and tossed her down on to the bed.

Dear God, she thought frantically as she twisted away, trying to cover herself with her hands. She had dressed—scented herself—for this moment. But not like this. Never like this…

She felt a sudden onrush of tears scald her face, and her voice cracked on a sob of sheer desolation as she echoed her own words aloud. 'Not like this—oh, please—not like this.'

And waited in agony to feel herself touched—taken.

But there was nothing. And when, at last, she dared look at him, he was standing over her, his arms folded across his chest, his mouth a hard, angry line in the bleak mask of his face.

'Stop crying,' he directed brusquely. 'You need not be concerned. I already despise myself for having wanted you at all.' He added with contempt, 'I shall not add to my own shame by taking you.'

She watched him walk in silence to the door. Saw it close behind him. Heard the heaviness of his footsteps descending the stairs and, a moment or two later, the Jeep's engine coming to life. Listened as the sound of it faded. Leaving—nothing.

Then Allie turned on to her stomach and began to weep in real earnest, her whole body shaking with her sobs.

As she began to mourn the love that had begun to fill her life, but which was now lost to her for ever.

* * *

It was several hours later that she heard the sound of another approaching vehicle. She'd come downstairs, principally to throw away her torn dress, and had remained. She was now occupying the corner of a sofa, in her dressing gown, hugging one of the cushions for comfort as she stared sightlessly into space. But at the noise she tensed, looking apprehensively towards the door.

It wasn't the Jeep coming back, she told herself, torn between relief and disappointment. But, even worse, it might be Solange, coming to gloat.

Then the door opened and Madelon Colville came in, walking slowly, leaning on a cane.

She saw Allie and checked instantly, her brows lifting in alarm as she registered the girl's pale, stricken face. *'Qu'as tu, mon enfant?'* she demanded urgently. 'What in heaven is the matter?'

'Remy.' Allie could only manage a choked whisper. She picked up the magazine and held it out, open at the appropriate page. 'Solange found—this. And showed him.'

*'Ah, ma petite.'* Tante took it from her, giving the offending photograph a cursory glance, then tossed it aside and sat beside her, taking the cold hands in hers. 'I always feared something like this.' She paused. 'Is he very angry?'

Allie looked at her with drowned eyes. 'Furious— and so bitter, because I didn't trust him enough to tell him the truth myself. I think he cared more about that than he did about Hugo,' she added wretchedly.

Tante nodded. 'And did you tell him how you had been trapped into this marriage, and how miserable it has made you?'

'I tried, but he didn't want to know.'

'*Eh bien.*' Tante patted her hand. 'In a day or two he will be calmer, and perhaps more ready to listen.' She paused thoughtfully. 'It is difficult for him in a community like this. He is a young, good-looking doctor. He falls in love with a single girl, and the whole town will come to the wedding and wish them well. But if he is known to be having an *affaire* with a married woman, that is a different matter.' She pursed her lips. 'Foolish as it seems, some husbands might not wish their wives to be treated by such a man.

'Besides,' she added candidly. 'His own sense of honour would balk at a liaison like that, I think.'

'Yes,' Allie agreed wanly. 'I—did get that impression.' She shook her head despairingly. 'Oh, God, I've been such a stupid, *criminal* fool. Why didn't I listen to you when you warned me?' She bit her lip. 'More importantly, why didn't I listen to Remy—and trust him?' Her voice broke. 'What am I going to do?'

'Tomorrow—nothing,' Tante said briskly. 'Except rest, and recover your looks and your spirits. Then go to see him, and tell him everything about your life in England. Make him aware of the whole truth about this ill-judged marriage, and explain why, for a little while, you wished to forget your unhappiness, however unwise it may have been. If he loves you, he will listen.'

Will he? Allie wondered. She found herself remembering his eyes, burning with angry contempt, mixed with pain. His words, 'I despise myself for having wanted you,' and had to control a shiver.

There had been moments when he'd reminded her of a wounded animal, she thought with anguish, and he might be equally dangerous to approach. Nevertheless, somehow, she had to try.

She leaned forward and kissed the older woman's scented cheek. 'It's wonderful to have you back,' she said gently. 'But you're still limping. Do you think you should have driven back from Vannes?'

Tante gave her a tranquil smile. 'They are the dearest friends,' she said. 'But sometimes—enough is enough.' She paused. 'Besides, *ma chère*, I woke this morning with a premonition that you would need me before the day was over.' She sighed. 'But I hoped very much I would be wrong.'

Allie slept badly that night, and spent the following day on tenterhooks, hoping against hope that Remy might relent in some way and contact her.

If he was just prepared to hear me out it would be something, she told herself silently, as she paced restlessly round the garden.

All the same, she knew that her failure to confide in him would still be a major stumbling block to any real *rapprochement* between them.

It was all he'd ever really asked of her, and she'd failed him totally. Which was something he might find impossible to forgive. And somehow she had to prepare herself for that. Even learn to accept it.

He may not want me any more, she thought desolately. Not after what I've done. But maybe—if I talk to him—explain how it was—we could at least part as friends.

Perhaps that's the most I can ask for. And the most I can offer.

When breakfast was over the next day, she came downstairs and said, 'I'm going to Trehel.'

Tante looked her over, assessing the elegant cut of the tailored cream linen trousers and the indigo silk of the short sleeved shirt Allie was wearing with them.

'With all flags flying, *petite*?' There was a touch of wryness in her voice.

Allie held up her left hand, with the gold band on its third finger. 'And total honesty at last.'

Tante nodded. 'The de Brizats are an old and a proud family, my child. Remember that, and do not expect this to be easy for you.' She paused. '*Bonne chance*, Alys.'

I'll need it, Allie thought as she started the car. Every scrap of luck that's going, and every prayer answered too.

Today, the house looked quiet and brooding in the sunlight, its shuttered windows like barriers, warning her not to come too close. Or was that her guilty conscience, working on her imagination?

Stomach churning, she drove round to the back and stopped in the courtyard. Remy's Jeep, she saw, was parked in its usual place, and she breathed a faint sigh of relief. At least she didn't have to go into Ignac and confront him at the medical centre.

As she got out, she heard the dogs begin to bark in the main house, but she ignored them. Squaring her shoulders, she marched up to the barn door and turned the handle, as she'd done so many times before. But the door didn't swing open to admit her, and she realised it must be locked.

He's never done that before, she thought with a silent sigh. Yet he must know that I'd be coming come to see him. He's obviously planning to make me beg.

She lifted the brass knocker shaped like a horse's head. They'd bought it together at the market only a few days ago, because she'd said the horse looked like Roland. She beat a vigorous tattoo.

But there was no response, nor sound of movement within. Allie stepped back, shading her eyes as she looked at the upper windows, and then with a rush and a whimper the dogs were there, circling round her, tails wagging, as they pushed delighted muzzles at her, waiting for her to stroke and pet them.

She turned and saw Georges de Brizat, standing looking at her across the courtyard, his face like a stone. He whistled abruptly, and the dogs, reluctant but obedient, moved back to his side. He hooked his hands into their collars and kept them there.

As if, she thought with real shock, she might contaminate them.

He said, 'Why are you here, *madame*? You must know you are not welcome.'

Allie lifted her chin. 'I need to see Remy. I have to talk to him—to explain.'

'It seems that your husband is the one who requires an explanation,' he said with grim emphasis. 'Go back to him, *madame*, if he will have you. There is nothing for you here.'

Her throat tightened. 'I won't go until I've seen Remy.'

'Then you will wait a very long time,' he said. 'He has gone.' And turned away.

'Gone?' Allie repeated the word almost numbly, then ran across the courtyard to him, catching at his sleeve, her voice pleading. 'Gone where? Please, Monsieur Georges, you must tell me…'

'Must?' the old man repeated, outrage in his voice. 'You dare to use that word to me, or any member of my family? And what obligation do I have to you, *madame*—the young woman who has ruined my grandson's life and, as a consequence, broken the heart of my son, too?'

She bent her head, hiding from the accusation in his eyes. 'I—I love Remy.'

'You mean that you desired him,' he corrected harshly. 'A very different thing.'

'No.' She forced her voice to remain level. 'I love him, and I want to spend my life with him.'

He was silent for a moment. 'But his wishes are entirely different, *madame*,' he said at last, his voice gruff. 'Yesterday he contacted the Paris headquarters of the medical charity he used to work for, and volunteered his services yet again. His father drove him to the train last night, having failed to persuade him to stay. By now he may be on his way to the other side of the world.

'And why?' His voice rose. 'Because he does not ever want to see you again, or hear your name mentioned. And for that he is prepared to sacrifice his home, his career, and all the dearest hopes of his family. He has gone, Alys, from all of us. From his whole life here. And even if I knew where I would not tell you. You have done enough damage.

'Now, leave, and do not come back. Because the answer here will always be the same.'

He moved to the back door, then halted, giving her one last, sombre look. 'It was a bad hour for my grandson when he saw you on the beach at Les Sables.'

'A very bad hour,' Allie said quietly. 'He would have done better to have left me to drown. Just as I'm dying now.'

And, stumbling a little, she went back to her car and drove away without a backward glance.

# CHAPTER NINE

SHE'D returned to England two days later, even though Madelon Colville, with sorrow in her eyes, had tried everything to dissuade her.

'You cannot go back, my child. To that house—that family,' she'd insisted. 'They will destroy you.'

'But I can't stay here either,' Allie had responded wearily. 'Not when I'm constantly surrounded by reminders of him. You must see that. And, anyway, nothing matters now. Not Hugo—or Grace. Any of them.' She tried to smile and failed. 'From now on they're the least of my troubles.'

It had been a different person who'd arrived back at Marchington—someone cool and remote, who had announced quietly but inflexibly that in future she would be occupying a bedroom of her own and did not expect to be disturbed there. Someone who had refused to be deflected from her purpose, no matter how many icy silences, shouting matches, or more subtle forms of persuasion she was subjected to.

She had faltered only once, when she'd been back just over a month and had begun to realise that the unexpected interruption to her body's normal rhythms was not caused by stress. That, in fact, she was going to have a baby.

A child, she'd thought, caught between shock and sudden exhilaration, a hand straying to her abdomen. Remy's child.

She had closed her eyes in a kind of thanksgiving. I have to tell him, she'd thought. He has to know straight away. Because when he does it will change everything. It has to…

She had shut herself away to telephone Trehel, and this time had spoken to Remy's father, Philippe de Brizat, only to encounter the same icy wall of hostility.

'How dare you force yourself on our attention again, *madame*? Have you not caused us all sufficient anguish?'

'Please, Dr de Brizat, I have to know where Remy is.' Her words tumbled over themselves. 'There's something I have to tell him urgently—something important. You must have a contact number or an address by now. Somewhere I can reach him.'

'For more messages of love?' His tone bit. 'He doesn't want to hear them. How many times must you be told? Anyway, he is in a remote part of South America, and communications are difficult. So let that be an end to it. Do not ask for him again.'

She heard him disconnect, and replaced her own receiver, pressing a clenched fist to her quivering lips. She sat like that for a long time, thinking. At last she got to her feet and went to Hugo. Expressionlessly, she told him she was pregnant, and waited for him to explode in rage.

But he didn't. For a moment his hands gripped the arms of his wheelchair so convulsively that the knuckles turned white, and then she saw him deliberately relax again. Lean back against his cushions. Even—dear God—smile at her.

'Darling,' he said warmly. 'That's wonderful news. The best ever. It's got to be a boy, of course—for Marchington. How soon can we find out definitely?'

She stared at him, astonished. Chilled. 'Hugo—don't you realize exactly what I've told you?'

'Naturally I do. I'm going to have a son and heir.' His tone was suddenly exultant. 'All my dreams have come true at last.' He shook his head. 'My mother's going to be so thrilled when I tell her.'

Your mother? Allie thought in total bewilderment. She's more likely to have me tarred, feathered and thrown out of the house to live in a cardboard box.

But once again she was proved completely wrong. Because Grace, when she broke the news to her, reacted with delight.

'It's what I've been praying for,' she said. 'Darling Hugo,' she added. 'How marvellous for him to be a father. This calls for champagne—although you won't be able to have any, Alice dear. The doctors these days say no alcohol during pregnancy, and we mustn't take any risks with your precious cargo.'

Allie stared at her, rigid with disbelief. 'Lady

Marchington,' she said. 'What are you talking about? You know quite well that Hugo—that he can't—'

'Don't be absurd, dear.' Grace Marchington's mouth was still smiling, but her eyes were slate-hard as they met Allie's, in a warning as explicit as it was uncompromising. 'Of course he can. He's your husband, and you've finally done your duty as his wife. It only took time and patience, as I always told him.' She became brisk. 'Now, let's have no more foolishness, and start to make plans. I know an excellent gynaecologist.'

Allie began to feel like that other Alice, who'd fallen down a rabbit hole and found herself in a parallel universe where nothing made any sense.

But, she told herself, that was only because, in spite of everything, she'd totally and frighteningly underestimated the Marchington obsession with having an heir.

What will they do if it's a girl? she wondered wryly. Have her exposed on a hillside?

But there seemed little point in fighting them—especially when her own mother also joined in the ludicrous pretence.

Besides, Allie soon realised she'd been wrong when she'd told Tante that nothing mattered any more. Because the baby—this little child, growing so rapidly inside her—suddenly became all that mattered, as did the need to provide him with food, warmth and shelter before and after his birth.

And if that meant becoming part of this weird conspiracy of silence, then she would do it. Because his own family didn't want to know.

'Whatever it takes, little one,' she whispered, her mouth twisting. 'Whatever it takes.'

As soon as the baby's sex was definitely established, the atmosphere at Marchington Hall grew almost feverish.

Deliberately, Allie created her own inner world, concentrating her energies on her baby's well-being, and acquiescing quietly with all the arrangements being made on his behalf.

She produced an all-purpose phrase—'Whatever you think best.'—which seemed to cover everything from the colour of the nursery walls to the re-emergence of Nanny who, up to then, had been pensioned off in a cottage in the grounds.

Allie wrote to Tante, giving her a guarded version of the truth—that she'd achieved a kind of reconciliation with Hugo.

Later, she wrote again, with the news of her pregnancy, and received a formal letter of congratulation, asking none of the questions she'd secretly dreaded. Allie could only guess whether or not her great-aunt had accepted her story.

At the same time it occurred to her that Hugo, at some point, would be bound to take his head unwillingly out of the sand and start to wonder about the baby's provenance.

We're behaving like people at a masquerade, she thought, but eventually the masks will have to come off—and what then? We have to introduce some reality here, and sooner rather than later.

For instance, she thought, almost clinically suppressing her own pang of anguish, Hugo needs to know that my child's real father was good and honourable, and came from a distinguished family.

And that, whatever may have happened afterwards, this child was made in love.

Although maybe that was too much information, she decided, wincing.

But, with the baby due to be born in a matter of weeks, it was certainly high time that she and her husband stopped pretending and had a serious talk about what had happened—preferably with no one else involved.

But when she finally nerved herself to approach Hugo she found him disinclined for conversation, complaining peevishly of a splitting headache. And she backed off, admitting to herself that he didn't look well.

The following day he was dead, and the subsequent post mortem revealed a massive brain haemorrhage.

The days that followed were largely a blur in her mind, until she stood in the churchyard, in a black tent-like coat that Grace had produced for her to wear, and thought that if one more person pressed her hand and told her in quavering tones how tragic it was that poor Hugo had not lived to see his child born she would probably go mad. Or else scream the truth at the top of her voice.

And then she looked across his grave, and met her

mother-in-law's icy, threatening gaze, and knew that, for the baby's sake, she would continue to remain silent.

And I've learned to live with my secret, Allie thought, her mouth twisting in self-loathing. To keep it well hidden and—pretend. To live a lie—just as I did so fatally with Remy. And—for Tom's sake—to compromise.

But no one can say I'm not being punished for my silence—past, present, and to come.

She got slowly up from the floor and went with lagging footsteps over to the bed, lying down on top of the covers, still fully dressed.

'And one day, if I live long enough,' she whispered, closing her eyes, 'I may be able to forgive myself. Even if no one else can.'

The room was brilliant with sunlight when she woke. She sat up, pushing her hair out of her eyes as she studied her watch, then yelped as she registered the time and realised that the morning was gone.

Tom's cot was empty, and neatly remade, she saw, as she grabbed a handful of fresh clothing and dashed to the bathroom. And she'd slept through it all.

She arrived downstairs in a flurry of embarrassed apology, but neither Tante nor Madame Drouac, busy at the sink, seemed to share her concern.

'You needed your sleep, *ma chère*,' Tante told her. 'And *le petit* has had his breakfast, also lunch, and is now perfectly contented.' She indicated the sofa, where Tom was slumbering among a nest of cushions.

'But you're the one who needs rest,' Allie protested anxiously. 'I'm supposed to be looking after you. That's why I came. Yet I'm just making more work.'

She was aware that Madame Drouac had turned, directing an openly curious look at Allie. She broke into a torrent of words, none of which Allie understood, apparently asking Tante a question, but Madelon Colville's brief reply accompanied by a shrug indicated that it wasn't too important.

'And now I have a plan,' her great-aunt announced, when Allie had obediently demolished a large bowl of chicken soup, thick with vegetables. 'For the remainder of the day, *chérie*, you must continue to relax. Take some time alone. Drive to Pont Aven, or perhaps Concarneau. Walk and breathe fresh air, to put colour back in your face and banish the shadows from your eyes. Look at shops and visit galleries, if you will. Do whatever seems good to you. And, above all, do not worry about anything. The little one will be quite safe here with us until you return.'

Allie saw that Madame Drouac was nodding vigorously and smiling, seemingly entranced at the idea of being in charge of an energetic toddler. All the same, she tried to protest, but was firmly overruled and almost bundled out to her car.

She began to see where Tom had acquired some of his self-will.

She thought of finding some quiet place and spreading the car rug in the sunshine, but realised suddenly she'd had enough of solitude. And that she didn't need more thinking time either.

Forcing herself to remember what had happened between Remy and herself had been a series of harsh, scarcely bearable agonies, but now that her unwilling journey into the past was over and done with she was conscious of an almost imperceptible lightening of the spirit.

It was, she thought, as if she'd performed some ritual of exorcism, so that her healing process could start. And maybe she had.

So there would be no more introspection, she warned herself. No more peeling away the layers to reveal her own guilt and unhappiness. That had to stop.

Now, she needed other people around—and plenty of them. So, in the end, she went to Concarneau, walking over the bridge to the old town and mingling with the hordes of tourists. Enjoying the holiday atmosphere.

There was a group of artists painting harbour scenes, and she stood for a while, watching them at work. She was seriously tempted by one of the paintings displayed for sale—as vivid and engaging as a cartoon. She was thinking of it for Tom's nursery wall, but common sense told her it would probably never survive Grace's inevitable disapproval.

Instead, she stopped at a stall selling beautifully made wooden toys—farm animals and birds mounted on little wheels and painted in radiantly cheerful colours. She chose a duck like a rainbow, a pink pig with black spots and, after a brief hesitation, a horse with piebald markings in brilliant red and white. She paid with a smile, imagining Tom trotting about dragging them behind him.

She sat outside a bar and drank lemon *pressé* in the sunshine, politely refusing an offer from a tall, blond Dane at the next table to share his bottle of wine.

Some children were watching a puppet show nearby, whooping with glee at what was clearly a familiar story, and Allie watched them, thinking of the time when Tom would be old enough to enjoy similar entertainments.

Not long now, she thought with a swift pang. How quickly time passes.

Which reminded her…

She'd enjoyed her afternoon, but now she needed to get back to Les Sables, because she'd left Tante to cope with Tom for quite long enough, even with Madame Drouac to assist her.

She found herself frowning a little as she walked back to the car. That was something else she had to deal with—the question of Tante's health. For a woman whose letter had implied she was sinking fast, Madelon Colville seemed remarkably robust, and certainly not someone just living out her last days.

I think a little plain talking on both sides is called for here, she decided, with a touch of grimness.

And even more of it would be needed when she eventually returned to Marchington Hall. Because her next task was to remove the upper hand over Tom's upbringing from its present custodians, and establish herself as the real authority.

She was her baby's mother, and there was nothing that Lady Marchington could say or do to prevent her. Not without risking the kind of challenge that Allie knew she would fight tooth and nail to avoid.

My first act, she told herself, will be to replace Nanny with someone young, sensible, and also *fun*, who'll work with me and not against me. And I really wish now that I'd bought that damned picture.

She was so busy planning her future campaign that she took the wrong road entirely and, cursing her own stupidity, had to draw in at the side of the road and consult her map. She'd need to retrace her route to get back to the coast, she realised crossly, unless she used what seemed a winding minor road to take her across country.

Well, it would be quicker, she reasoned, restarting the car. And she'd have to concentrate on her driving, rather than scoring imaginary points from Grace, which would be no bad thing.

It was only when she'd gone more than halfway that she realised her road wandered past the other side of the stone circle where Remy had taken her on that first afternoon, and they were there, only a few hundred yards to her right, their dark shapes crowning the faint rise of the ground.

Shocked, Allie found herself braking for no fathomable reason, then fumbled her gears, stalled the engine and swore.

She sat for a moment, gripping the wheel and steadying her breathing. It went without saying that the rational course was to drive on and not look back.

But was that because, in spite of her brave resolution, she still dared not face all of her memories? Would she always wonder, in fact, if she'd simply taken the coward's way out?

Well, there's only one way to discover the truth, she thought, undoing her seat belt. And if I can bear this, I'll know that I can stand anything.

She walked across the short scrubby grass without hurrying, telling herself with every step that she could always turn back, but knowing that she wouldn't.

She entered the ring of tall stones and stood in the middle of them, lifting her face to the sun. Wine, she thought, and strawberries. Kisses that drew the soul out of her body. The warm, calculated arousal of his hands. The day when her self-created myth of cool reserve had crumbled, awakening her body to the bewildering force of its own desires—the sweet vulnerability of passion.

Oh, no, she thought, drawing a swift, painful breath. She'd forgotten nothing. How could you ignore the time when your life had changed for ever? Pretend it had never happened?

Or even, she realised, as her heart suddenly missed a beat, make believe that she was still alone here. That every instinct she possessed was wrong, and no tall figure had emerged from the shelter of the stones behind her.

She turned slowly and looked at him across the pool of sunlit grass.

He seemed, she thought, to have been carved from granite himself, the lines of cheekbone and jaw sharply delineated, the mouth set bleakly. He was wearing khaki pants and a black shirt, open at the throat, the sleeves turned back over brown forearms.

He was also, she realised, thinner, and a century older. She hadn't realised that when she'd seen him in Ignac, because he'd been smiling as he dealt with old Madame Teglas. But he was not smiling now.

The blue eyes glittered like chips of ice as he watched her, letting the silence stretch endlessly between them. Rigidly maintaining his distance.

Allie tried to speak—to say his name—to say something—but her voice wouldn't obey her. All she could do was wait helplessly for him to take the initiative.

Which, at long last, he did.

'I was told you had returned.' His voice was expressionless. 'But I did not think it could be true.'

She squared her shoulders defensively. 'Bad news clearly travels fast. But I didn't know you were back in Brittany either. I thought—I understood that you were still in South America.'

His mouth twisted. 'Or you would not have come back?' he countered harshly.

'No,' she said. 'I would not.'

There was another silence. 'I also hear that you are a widow now.' The words seemed wrenched from him. 'A rich widow—with a baby. So you managed to achieve some kind of *rapport* with the husband you professed not to love, *hein*? Tell me something. Did he know—about us?'

'Yes,' she said, dry-mouthed. 'He knew.' *Knew, but never acknowledged—never admitted the truth.*

'And, of course, he accepted your betrayal of him. Took you back again into your rich and comfortable life as if nothing had happened.

She shrugged, trying to erase the scorn in his voice. 'Why not? All life is a series of compromises. As I'm sure you've discovered for yourself,' she added, her mind wincing away from the thought of Solange Geran.

And she saw him move for the first time, suddenly, restlessly, taking a step forward. He said quietly, 'What are you doing here, Alys?'

'I had a letter from my great-aunt. It made me—concerned for her.' She lifted her chin. 'As you of all people should realise.' *After all, you're her doctor now, so you must know…*

'And Tante Madelon is very dear to me,' she added curtly. 'I don't want to lose her.'

Remy raised his brows. 'You feel that is a possibility?' He sounded almost curious.

'I don't know.' She shook her head. 'Although she sent for me, she seems—reluctant to discuss the situation.'

'Well, that is hardly strange,' he said. 'Under the circumstances.'

'I suppose so.' Allie bit her lip. 'So, will you explain it all to me—please?'

'I regret that is impossible.' The hardness was back

in his voice. 'But give *madame* time, and she will tell you what you need to know.'

She stared at him. 'And that's all you have to say?'

'On that subject, yes.' He nodded. '*Madame* does not wish me, or anyone, to speak for her.' He paused. 'But if you are so anxious about her, why are you not with her, at Les Sables, instead of here—in this place—at this time?'

He took another step, narrowing the distance between them. 'Did you come to count the stones, perhaps? To see if one more had been added—for you?'

Allie threw back her head. 'I hardly think your saint would interest himself in our little *affaire*.' She paused. 'If it comes to that, what are *you* doing here?'

'I had to call at the Teglas farm, to attempt to resolve a problem.'

'You mean you're now expected to be a mediator as well as a doctor?' She raised her eyebrows. 'How bizarre.'

'On occasion. But I am not always successful.' For a moment his face was rueful. 'How can one reconcile two women who hate each other?'

Her throat tightened. 'You can't—especially if they are fighting over a man. Eventually one will win. The other will lose. That's—life.'

'So,' he said slowly. 'Where is the compromise there?'

'I didn't say it worked in every case.' She shrugged. 'I was just—fortunate.'

'And now fortune has brought you back here,' he said. 'Why?'

She bit her lip. 'Tante Madelon sent me out for an hour or two. I was on the way home, but I took the wrong road, and found myself passing this place. That's all.'

'*Vraiment?*' The blue eyes met hers—held them mockingly. 'Now, I have another theory. I think that, like myself, you have been drawn back here because you are unable to keep away.'

'That's absurd.'

'Is it? Then why have I always been so sure that one day, if I waited long enough, I would find you here?' His smile was like a scar. 'It is—almost amusing, *n'est-ce pas?*'

She made herself look away, aware that her heart-beat had quickened. 'My sense of humour seems to have deserted me. And, whatever your own motiva-tion, I'm here solely because I made a silly mistake.'

'You were passing,' he said. 'You could have driven on. But you did not.'

'An impulse,' Allie said shortly. 'Which I now se-riously regret.'

'At last the truth,' Remy said softly. 'Or as close to it as I can expect from you, my cheating witch. And you will have more cause for repentance when I have done with you, believe me.'

Allie felt suddenly as if the stones were closing in on her—caging her with him in this isolated place.

'Don't,' she said with difficulty. 'Please…'

'You seem nervous, *ma belle*,' he gibed. Suddenly he was within touching distance, and her pulses were quickening—threatening to run out of control—and not simply because she was scared.

'Yet what can I possibly do to you that I have not done many times before, hmm? That you have not welcomed, begged for more,' he added with hurtful insolence.

*I have to get away from here. I have to get away now...*

Allie moved backwards, only to find her retreat blocked by the bulk of one of the great stones, directly behind her. She leaned back against it, suddenly needing its support, because her legs were shaking. She stared up at him, her eyes pleading, her voice uneven. 'That's not how it was. You make it sound— crude. And cruel.'

'Ah, *je m'excuse, madame.*' His tone jeered at her. '*L'adultère—c'est si spirituel, n'est-ce pas? Et si gentil.*'

He rested his hands each side of her on the sun-warmed rock, so that she was in his arms, but not held there.

'So,' he said quietly. 'Give me one good reason, Alys, why I should not treat you like the whore you are.'

'Because it's all in the past, Remy,' she whispered desperately. 'It has to be. We both have—different lives now. And I—I think I've been punished enough.'

'Punishment?' His brows lifted. 'What a hypocrite you are.'

He bent his head, and his mouth took hers. Not gently. Almost brutally, in fact.

But what else did she expect? asked a dying voice inside her head. There were two years of anger and bitterness tied up in that kiss, and an infinity of loneliness and guilt in her own aching surrender to it.

He was out for revenge, and she knew it.

Yet desire, for her, was instant, unthinking. The appeasement of an emptiness that went far beyond her physical being. Her hands tangled in his dark hair, holding him to her, while her lips parted for him. He pushed up her top and she felt his hands on her bare breasts, her nipples lifting at his touch, aching with remembered sweetness.

She felt the hard, heated pressure of his erection against her thighs, and moaned her need into his open mouth, as sky, earth and grey stone swung round her in a dizzying arc.

She raised a bent knee, hooking it round his hip, pushing herself urgently against him. And if she was the beggar he'd called her, she didn't care. Because she wanted him inside her so badly that nothing else mattered. Because she longed to be entered—to be filled. To be made complete again by the only man she would ever love.

And, just before they spiralled out of control into mutual and rapturous oblivion, she wanted to hear him say that he loved her too…

Only he hadn't spoken of love. The thought rose from her reeling mind with sudden and terrible clarity. He'd spoken instead of sex, and satiation. Called her a cheat and a whore, who'd give him whatever he wanted.

*I despise myself for wanting you.* Those chilling

words of parting that had haunted her so often during the past long months. How could she have forgotten them?

Because he'd meant them then. And all the evidence indicated that he still meant them now.

And if she let him take her like this, without tenderness or respect—use her to satisfy a physical need as if she were nothing more than a cup of water for a parched throat—then she would despise herself too.

Shame had nearly destroyed her before. She could not let it happen again, not when there was Tom who needed her. Oh, God, *Tom*...

She tore her mouth from his, pushing frantically at his chest, muttering the word 'no' over and over again, until her voice rose almost to a scream.

*'Tais toi. Sois tranquille.'* Remy captured her wrists, holding her clenched fists away from him. 'What is the matter with you?'

'It's over—that's the matter.' Her voice was thick—uneven. 'Now, let go of me, damn you.'

He made no move to release her, so she wrenched herself free, taking a few shaky steps before she sank down on the grass, wrapping her arms round her body as she tried to recover her breath.

When she could look at him, he was sitting on the grass a few feet away. He said quietly, 'What is this?'

'You can really ask that?' She pushed her hair out of her eyes, glaring at him. 'Well, it's quite simple. I'm paying for no more bloody mistakes—do you hear me? This time I'm the one that's walking away—for good.'

'You did not give that impression,' Remy said slowly. 'A moment ago.'

She shrugged. 'You caught me off guard. And you were always terrific in bed,' she added, with deliberate insouciance. 'So for that moment I was tempted. But not any more.'

He said icily, 'Now you are the one who is crude.'

'I'm so sorry. But you won't be distressed by my coarseness for much longer.' She lifted her chin defiantly. 'Because I've finally learned my lesson. Brittany is poison to me, and I'm going back to England just as soon as it can be arranged. What's more, I'm going to persuade Tante Madelon to go too.'

He'd wrenched up a handful of grass and was studying it as if it contained a clue to the universe, but his head lifted sharply at that.

'You think she will do so?' There was an odd note in his voice.

'Why not?' Allie demanded curtly. 'She'll have a better life with me. I'll make sure she has every comfort—everything she wants.' *For whatever time she has left...*

'Of course,' he said softly. 'Your money. The great panacea, solving all problems, healing all wounds. But my family are not paupers either.'

'I'm sure,' she said. *After all, Solange is a practical girl, looking for a better life. Would she have wanted you for your eyes—your smile alone, I wonder? Or even your skill as a lover? I doubt it.*

She shook herself mentally, hurrying into speech.

'Not that it makes any difference. And from now on, until I leave, I'll do my damnedest to stay out of your way. So perhaps you'll extend the same courtesy to me.'

'You really think it is that simple?' His tone bit as he flung away the grass. 'Alys, forget what has just happened here. It was—wrong.'

She wondered if he had suddenly remembered Solange and his new obligations, and felt something freeze inside her.

'But there are things that need to be said,' he went on.

'Perhaps.' She kept her voice flat. 'But not by us. Or to each other. The time for that is long past. I have a better idea. Why don't we both just—stop? Once and for all, here and now?'

There was a silence, then he said politely, *'D'accord*—if that is what you want. I hope you are not suggesting that we—part as friends.'

'No,' she said tautly. 'That would hardly be appropriate. I'll simply—return to my car, and let you go to yours.' As he rose lithely to his feet, she got up too, smoothing her crumpled skirt with hands that were still unsteady. She could only hope he wouldn't notice.

*Keep the conversation going. Make it all sound normal. As if you aren't dying inside.*

She paused. 'Or did you ride here?' she asked with ghastly brightness. She glanced about her. 'Although I don't see Roland.'

'Roland went to a new owner in the Auvergne,' he said harshly. 'I too had no plans to return, *tu comprends.'*

'Remy—no.' She was startled into open distress.

'But you loved him…' Her voice faded awkwardly as she realised what she was saying.

'Please do not disturb yourself.' His voice was cold. 'I have survived greater losses, believe me, and even their memory fades in time.' He stepped back, making her a slight ironic bow. 'I wish you well, *madame. Adieu.*'

She turned, walking out of the circle, trying not to look as if she was in a hurry, or anything but fully in control of herself and the situation.

Aware, with every step she took, that he was watching, but not daring to look back.

Telling herself, as the distance between them lengthened, that she'd done the right thing at last. Absolutely the right thing—for everyone.

And trying desperately to believe it.

# CHAPTER TEN

ALLIE drove back to Les Sables, trying to use the same steely care she would have accorded to the presence of thick fog or black ice. She had to appear calm and composed, she told herself. As if that final encounter with Remy had never happened.

Because it would only distress Tante Madelon if she discovered even an atom of the truth—especially when the older woman had tried so hard to warn her that she had nothing to hope for.

What a fool I've been, Allie castigated herself bitterly. What a pathetic abysmal fool.

Did I ever—in my wildest dreams—think that Remy's attitude to me might have mellowed over the past months and several thousand miles? Did I believe in some empty corner of my heart that he would really be able to forgive me for betraying him like that?

Well, the answer to that was—yes. She'd probably done exactly that. But, then, she'd been able to indulge any sad fantasy she liked when she'd existed in the absolute certainty that she was never going to see him again.

But now she'd walked headlong into hard reality, and it had left her broken and reeling.

So much so that she took the next corner faster and wider than she'd intended, and received a bad-tempered blare on the horn from a vehicle travelling rapidly in the other direction.

However, it was only when she glanced in the mirror, berating herself for her stupid lapse in concentration, that she realised it was a blue pick-up.

Not that she should read anything into that, she thought. There must be dozens of the things around, and they couldn't all belong to Solange Geran. That glancing impression of a flash of silver-blonde hair as the truck had erupted past her was probably just a figment of her imagination. And so was the fleeting sense of something hostile and malignant aimed at her from the other vehicle, like a stone thrown through her window.

At least she hoped so. Because even the briefest glimpse of the girl who'd destroyed her life would be altogether too much to bear.

Although she was being unfair, and she knew it. She'd laid the charges for her own destruction. Solange had merely lit the fuse.

It was the thought of her wearing Remy's ring, queening it over her little domain at Trehel, that was piercing Allie's soul like an open wound.

He has to marry someone, she acknowledged wretchedly. The celibate lifestyle would have no attraction for Remy, and that enormous bed was intended for sharing. But—dear God—does it have to be Solange? Does she have to triumph quite so completely?

The road ahead of her blurred suddenly, and she pulled over on to the verge, putting her head down on the steering wheel as she fought the misery of loss that was tearing her apart.

But there's nothing I can do, she told herself, choking back a sob. Remy has gone, and it's all my own fault. I have no one to blame but myself. If I'd trusted him, been honest, Solange could have done nothing.

When she finally arrived back at Les Sables, she'd regained a measure of self-command. She sat for a long moment, arranging her face into a controlled and smiling mask. Trying to look like someone who'd enjoyed a relaxed and pleasant afternoon.

But when she walked into the living room and Tom greeted her with a toothy grin and an exultant word that was undoubtedly *'Maman'*, while Tante and Madame Drouac beamed with pride in the background, she was rocked to her foundations.

What will he learn next? she wondered, with sudden shock. To say Papa? And she felt her throat thicken with swift tears as she hung on to her self-control like grim death.

But she managed it with the help of the new toys, which her son accepted with wide-eyed delight, and supper was a determinedly cheerful affair, as she coaxed him to repeat the 'M' word, praising his latest accomplishment with suitable extravagance.

Although she might be overdoing the hilarity, she

realised, suddenly encountering a shrewdly questioning look from Tante.

When the meal was over, and she'd mopped the bathroom floor after Tom's boisterous bedtime romp in the tub, Allie came slowly downstairs.

Tante was on the sofa, knitting a Tom-sized sweater in thick blue wool, her fingers rapid, her hands held low in her lap in the Continental manner that Allie had never mastered.

'He is asleep?'

'Yes, but he went down fighting all the way.' Allie sat beside her, nerving herself for another battle. She took a deep breath. 'Darling, this afternoon gave me a real chance to think. Quite soon now, I'll have to return to England, and I'd—really like you to go with me.'

The busy hands instantly stilled. 'Go to England?'

Tante couldn't have sounded more shocked, Allie thought, if she'd suggested setting up a naturist camp in the Arctic Circle.

'Please listen,' she urged. 'It's not that outlandish a scheme. You won't tell me what's the matter with your health, but your letter clearly implied that it's something serious, and I think we should get a second opinion—before it's too late.'

Madelon Colville was staring at her almost raptly. 'Go on, *ma mie*.'

Allie swallowed. 'And while this house is gorgeous, and I can see why you love it here, and might want to stay until...' She floundered over the unthinkable, then recovered. 'What I'm trying to say is that it's still pretty isolated, even with Madame Drouac to look after you.'

'Yes,' her great-aunt surprisingly agreed. 'That has become—a consideration.'

'Well, there's a really good cottage near the Hall. Hugo had it completely renovated for his groom, just before the accident. Everything's on the ground floor, so there are no stairs to cope with. It could be—perfect.'

'There is, however, your *belle-mère*.' Tante's tone was dry. 'Who might not welcome a Breton invasion of her property.'

'The estate belongs to Tom,' Allie said. 'Grace is only one of his trustees. I can deal with her.'

'You sound very brave, *ma chère*.'

Allie forced a smile. 'I had to wake up some time.' She paused. 'Well, what do you think of my idea?'

'It is a kind, good thought,' Tante said gently. 'But I have no wish to live in England again.'

'But you need to be looked after,' Allie pleaded. 'There must be treatment of some kind…'

Madelon Colville sighed. '*Mon enfant*, I am not ill. Just no longer young.'

'But your letter…'

Her great-aunt took her hand, patted it. 'I told you that this would be my last summer at Les Sables. And so it will. In the autumn, I plan to sell and move—elsewhere.'

'But I thought…'

'That I was dying?' The older woman shook her head. '*Au contraire, chérie.* I have every reason to live, even at my advanced age.'

'You—deceived me?' Allie felt dazed.

*'Une petite ambiguité, peut-être,'* Tante agreed calmly. 'Because, selfishly, I wished very much to see you, and also *le petit*, before more time passed. And for that I needed a very good reason. One that you would believe, and which would defeat the undoubted objections of *madame ta belle-mère.'* She paused. 'Was it not so?'

'Oh, yes.' Allie was still gasping. 'It certainly worked.'

'Then what harm has been caused?'

Oh, God, thought Allie. If you knew—if you only knew...

'And am I forgiven?' There was an anxious note in Tante's voice.

'Of course you are, darling.' Allie tried to speak lightly. 'So what shall I say when I go back? That the moment you saw me you made a lightning recovery?'

Tante's eyes were gravely questioning. 'Must you—go back, *ma petite*?'

'I have to.' Allie stared at the floor. *Where else is there for me to go? Because God knows I can't stay here.* 'After all, Marchington is Tom's home,' she went on, trying to sound positive. 'I—I can't keep him away for too long.'

'But he also has Breton blood,' Tante said. 'Another important heritage.'

And one that I dare not tell him about, thought Allie, her throat tightening.

She pinned on a smile. 'But you haven't told me yet where you're planning to live after this?'

Tante was vague. 'Oh, I have not yet made a final decision.' She yawned. 'There is no great urgency.'

And no pressing reason for me to stay either, Allie told herself as she lay in bed that night. But Tante would be terribly disappointed if I left before the end of the week, especially as I know I'll never be able to come back again. Or not with Tom, anyway. The risk is far too great.

So I'll return to England as planned, but until I go I'll just have to stay firmly around Les Sables. That way, there's no possibility of meeting Remy again. Or anyone else I'd prefer to avoid.

Because, looking back, she was almost certain that it *had* been Solange driving the blue pick-up that afternoon.

And if I saw her, she may well have seen me, she thought grimly.

She sighed to herself. She should never have come here, she thought with quiet desolation.

Nothing had turned out as she'd expected. And, while she was eternally grateful that Tante wasn't suffering from some life-threatening condition, she couldn't understand why the older woman hadn't immediately put her mind at rest.

She knew what I was thinking, so why didn't she tell me? she wondered. And what is she still not saying now? Or am I just being paranoid?

She sighed again, and turned her mind to the immediate future. She had to admit that returning to Marchington Hall held no attraction for her, and nor did the inevitable battles with her mother-in-law that lay ahead. But they'd be worth it, she told herself determinedly, if they secured for Tom the happy childhood he deserved, rather than Grace's rigid regime. She had to believe that, because she had nothing else to cling to. Nothing to hope for either.

So she would go back and take her rightful place as the new, improved Lady Marchington. She would concentrate her energies on fighting Grace and winning, and forget there'd ever been a girl who'd found Paradise in a man's arms and dared to dream of a different life.

And when these final days that she would ever spend in Brittany were over, she would ensure that, whatever her own feelings, she left only happy memories behind her.

'I am going to the hairdresser in Ignac,' Tante announced over lunch the next day. 'Do you wish to accompany me, *chérie*? You have shopping, perhaps?'

Allie pretended to consider the proposal. 'Not really—and I think, if you don't mind, that Tom would be much happier playing in the garden,' she returned, then suddenly smiled. 'Do you know, he insisted on having all his new animals in bed with him last night?'

Tante smiled too. 'He is an enchanting child, Alys. But he needs a masculine influence in his life—a father figure.' She gave her great-niece a penetrating look. 'I hope the disaster of your first husband has not turned you against the idea of a suitable remarriage.'

Allie shrugged. 'Perhaps—one day. But I don't meet

that many people, and besides it would take a very
brave man to get past Grace and the hedge of thorns
she's built round Marchington to enshrine Hugo's
memory.' She pulled a self-deprecating face. 'I think
most guys would prefer a more accessible woman.'

'A problem.' Madelon Colville finished her last
morsel of cheese and rose. 'But perhaps you should
attend first to the thorn hedge around your own heart,
*ma chère*,' she said gently. 'Then all else might follow.'

And left Allie gasping.

It was a gloriously hot afternoon. Allie, bikini-clad,
lay on the rug, propped on an elbow as she watched
her son playing, pushing his animals around on the
grass with ferocious concentration, quacking and
mooing at what he felt were appropriate moments.

Sometimes, she thought tenderly, he even got it right.

Wearing only his nappy, and an over-large cotton
hat, he looked like an adorable if grubby mushroom.
And he was happy. Also a little too pink, Allie thought,
sitting up and reaching for the high-factor cream.

But Tom was enjoying himself too much to stand
still while she applied it, and set up a wail of protest,
his wriggles dislodging the sunhat.

'You'll have good reason to cry if you get burned,'
she warned him with mock severity as he tried to pull
away from her. Then suddenly he was still, his attention apparently riveted by something over Allie's
shoulder, his thumb going to his mouth as it did when
there were strangers about and he felt shy.

*Strangers.* There was a sudden tingle between her shoulderblades, and she felt the fine hairs lift on the nape of her neck.

Even before she looked round, Allie knew who was there. Who it had to be.

She hadn't heard his approach. He'd simply arrived as he always had in the past, skirting the side of the house unannounced. And now he was standing there, just a few feet away, his hands clenched into fists at his sides as he stared at them both.

Allie was in shock. Instinctively she drew Tom closer, her grip tightening, startling a small indignant yowl from him.

She said 'What—what are you doing here? What do you want?'

His voice was hoarse, almost unrecognisable. 'I— I came—because…'

His gaze was fixed on Tom. He looked like someone who had suddenly turned to find himself face to face with his own reflection in a mirror. She saw a muscle move convulsively in his throat.

Dry-mouthed, she said, 'Remy, I'd like you to leave.'

Instead, it was Tom who moved, his small, slippery body evading her slackened clasp as he set off across the grass towards the tall, silent newcomer, grabbing a handful of denim trouser leg to steady himself, and laughing up into the rigid face above him.

And Remy bent, lifting him into his arms and holding him there, his eyes closed and a tanned cheek pressed against the small dark head.

She was trembling violently as she stretched out her arms. 'Remy,' she said huskily. 'Remy—give him to me—please.'

She realised that she was kneeling, what it must look like, and scrambled to her feet, wishing desperately that she had slightly more covering than a few square inches of black fabric.

She said again, 'Remy…' And her voice broke on his name.

There was an endless, breathless pause. She could hear the thunder of her own heart. Then he raised his head slowly and looked at her, and she took a pace backwards, recoiling from what she saw in his eyes, putting up her hands as if to ward him off, although he hadn't taken a step.

His voice was quiet. 'So I have a son.' He paused. 'And when, precisely, *madame*, did you plan to tell me this?'

She felt sick with fear, and a mixture of other emotions, but she managed to lift her chin defiantly. 'I didn't.'

'Ah,' he said. 'A little honesty at last. I congratulate you.'

'Because,' she said, 'I thought I'd never see you again—if you remember?'

'I have forgotten nothing. I recall in particular that you *did* see me, only yesterday.'

'Yes.' Allie set her jaw.

'And still you did not tell me.' The statement simmered with pent-up anger.

'No.'

'But why? Why did you not speak?' His voice rose, and Tom lifted his head from the curve of his father's shoulder.

'Maman…' he whimpered.

'We're frightening him.' Allie put out a hand. 'Give him back to me, please.'

'He is also tired,' Remy said curtly. 'But you are right. He should not be here—for this. Show me where he sleeps.'

Allie hesitated, then reluctantly led the way into the house.

*We were lovers, and you used to carry me up these stairs to this very room. Now you're carrying our child, and we're enemies.*

For a moment Remy paused on the threshold as he recognised where they were, and she saw his face harden as he glanced fleetingly towards the bed.

Then he recovered himself and walked forward. He put Tom gently down in the cot, in spite of his drowsily bad-tempered objections, murmuring to him softly in his own language until the little boy seemed to accept the situation, his thumb returning to his mouth.

Allie turned away, feeling her throat tighten as she grabbed almost blindly for her robe and put it on. She couldn't afford to be half-naked in front of him. It made her vulnerable, and for this confrontation she needed all the barriers she could get, she thought, hastily knotting the sash round her waist.

Remy looked round as he straightened—and she

moved hurriedly towards the door, stumbling a little as her foot caught in the trailing hem of her robe.

His mouth curled contemptuously. 'You are trembling, *madame*. You think you are in some kind of danger? That I want, perhaps, to kill you for what you have done?'

'No.' There were, she thought, far worse things than death. Abruptly she left the room, leading the way downstairs and out once more into the small furnace of the garden. Where she faced him, eyes wary, hands clenched beside her.

'What is his name?' The question was almost conversational in tone, but she wasn't deceived.

'Thomas,' she said clearly. 'Thomas Marchington. *Sir* Thomas, if you want to be strictly accurate.'

His brows snapped together. 'He has your husband's title?'

'Yes,' she said. 'And the house, and the land, and the money. He—he's a very wealthy little boy.'

*'Mon Dieu.'* He whispered the words. For a moment he was silent, then he said slowly, as if the words were being torn from him in some terrible way, 'So you deliberately deceived this man—your husband—you let him think the baby was his—for gain—?'

'No.' She cut across him, her voice shaking. 'I didn't—I swear it. You have to believe me.'

'Why should I believe anything you say?'

She swallowed. 'There isn't a reason in the world, and I know that. But Hugo—couldn't have a child of his own. Not after his accident. He knew it, but because he wanted an heir—a son for Marchington—he wouldn't admit it. Ever.'

She looked away. 'Instead, he said it was my fault. Because I didn't know what to do in bed—how to perform the miracle that would finally arouse him and make me pregnant. Only it was—impossible. And he hated me for it.'

She ran her tongue round her dry lips. 'Eventually, I was at desperation point—worn out with being ignored all day—and then, at night, having to deal with his anger and frustration—the names he called me. I—I had to get away.'

'And so you came here, and found me.' His short laugh was like the lash of a whip across her senses. 'A willing stud to solve the little problem with your bloodline, *enfin*.'

'No-o-o!' It was a tortured sound, wrung from the depths of her. 'It wasn't like that. It was never like that.'

'We had unprotected sex, Alys, because you told me that there was no problem.' His voice was inimical. 'That was another lie.'

She looked at him incredulously. 'You mean you were just enquiring if I was on the Pill?' She pressed her hands against burning cheeks. 'I—I didn't understand. I thought stupidly that you were asking if you'd hurt me—if I wanted you to go on.'

'A convenient mistake for someone who needed so badly to have a baby.'

'Yes,' she said. 'Perhaps so—if I'd been thinking that clearly. But I wasn't. You see—it was the dream.'

'What is this?' he asked harshly. 'Another excuse?'

'I don't think I even know any longer.' Ally turned away, leaning against the trunk of the tree, feeling the bark scraping her skin through the thin robe. One pain, she thought, to cancel out another. 'But, that's how it seemed then—being with you—being happy and loved. Loving you so much I thought I'd die with the joy of it. And feeling safe—from that other dreadful existence. From Hugo and his mother, and everything waiting for me back in England.'

She stared down at the grass. 'I knew I should tell you that I was married, but that would have forced me to face reality again. And I—I didn't want my dream to end. It was too precious. The one marvellous, shining thing in the mess I'd made of my life, and I was terrified I'd lose it—that I'd lose you.'

Her laugh cracked in the middle. 'And then I did anyway. But at least I had my memories—everything you'd said—everything you'd done. Or that's what I told myself—until I realised I was going to have a baby.'

'And still you said nothing.' His voice was grim. 'Sent me no word.'

'I wanted to.' She didn't tell him about the phone call to Trehel, his father's dismissal of her. What good could it do now? she thought wearily. Just make more trouble. 'But you were thousands of miles away, gone from my life for ever, or so I thought. I had to assume sole responsibility for our child. And part of that was being honest with Hugo. I went to him—told him I was pregnant, fully expecting that he'd throw me out—divorce me. But instead he—he just—pretended that the baby was his. That I'd finally done my duty by the family. And by him. That everything was perfect.'

'And you allowed this?' He was incredulous. 'You—went along with this delusion?'

'I had a choice,' she said stonily. 'To struggle as a single parent or know that my child would be brought up with every material advantage—his security guaranteed for his entire life.'

She bent her head. 'He was all I had, Remy, and I—I wanted the best for him. At the time it seemed—the right thing to do.'

'The *right thing*?' His voice bit. 'To let him live a lie? Or did you plan to tell him one day that he had a real father—a true family?'

'You want the truth?' She turned to face him, eyes glittering in her white face. 'I don't know, Remy. I just don't know. That's something I'll have to decide when the time comes.'

'The time is already here, Alys.'

'What do you mean? He's far too young. He couldn't possibly understand.'

'You are the one who must understand,' he said, and his voice chilled her to the bone. 'Thomas is my son, *madame*, and I want him. And this English estate and its money, and the title, can all go to hell. Because the lying stops now.'

The blue eyes burned into her. 'Our child will stay here, Alys. With me. Where he belongs.'

There was a stunned silence, then she said

hoarsely, 'No, Remy. You don't mean that. You—
you can't...'

'And who will stop me?'

'I shall,' she said. 'And Lady Marchington. Do you
really think she'll let her grandchild go? She'll fight
you every step of the way—and she can afford it, even
if it goes to court. Because that's what it will mean.
Down to the wire.'

He looked at her scornfully. 'You think I cannot
match her? You are wrong, Alys. My mother was her
father's only child, and he was a very rich man.
Through her, his money has now come to me. I work
in medicine because I wish, not because I must.

'But it will never come to court,' he added. 'The
simplest DNA test will prove my son's paternity. This
lady will not proceed, because she will not wish the
truth to be known. And nor, I think, will you.'

'But what about you?' She spread impassioned
hands in a pleading gesture. 'I admit—I never meant
you to know. Because—yes—I was afraid of what
you might do. But also I couldn't see what good it
could possibly achieve.'

'Are you quite mad?'

'No,' she said. 'I'm trying to be sane—for both of
us.' She paused. 'Oh, Remy—think. What will people
say—how will they react—your family—your patients—when they discover you have an illegitimate
son? The—the wife you may take in the future. What
about her? Will—will she want to take on the responsibility of another woman's child?'

*Solange—Solange would not even be kind. Instinct told her that.*

She tried again. 'Wouldn't it be better to leave things as they are? I'll be leaving soon. Can't we please stop hurting each other and get on with our lives?'

'It is kind of you to concern yourself with my reputation, *madame*,' Remy said coldly. 'But I find the well-being of my son infinitely more important than any local gossip. And, for the moment, I have no wife.'

She took a step forward. 'Remy, If you take Tom, then I'll have nothing left in the world.'

'Then you too will know what that is like.' His tone was bleak. 'How it was for me, out in that stinking rainforest, lying awake at night, not knowing whether I would ever see another day's dawn, and realising I did not care. Because I had nothing left either, Alys. You took it all.

'And when I returned I heard that you had had a child—that you had carried another man's seed inside you. I thought that was bad, but now I know the truth—and that, believe me, is so much worse.'

He added quietly, 'So this time, Alys, it is I who will take everything—from you.'

'What do you want me to do,' she asked tonelessly. 'Go down on my knees and beg?'

'And after that—what?' His brows lifted. 'The offer of your body, perhaps? After all, it would not be the first time—in this garden you have given yourself to me. It might even be here that Thomas was made. That would have a certain irony, I think.'

He saw the colour rush into her pale face, the uncertainty in her eyes, and his smile was mocking.

'*Alors, ma belle,* what do you say?'

'Is—is that what you want?' She stared down at the grass.

He gave a slight shrug. 'I could, perhaps, be tempted.'

Her hands went slowly to her sash, fumbling with the knot until it was loose. She shrugged the robe off her shoulders and let it fall.

*Not the first time, no. But always before it was part of the dream. Whereas everything had changed now. They were different people. And this—this was brutal, mind-numbing reality.*

The silence around them seemed suddenly heavy— pulsating.

Allie unhooked the top of her bikini. Removed it.

It occurred to her that she'd never had to do this before. Not stand in front of him and—simply strip. Being undressed by him—kissed and caressed out of her clothes—had always been part of the pleasure. She realised that even now she was expecting him to move—to come to her and take her in his arms. Complete the task for her...

Only he didn't. And somehow she found she dared not even look at him.

Awkwardly, she slid down the tiny briefs and stepped out of them.

Stood, arms at her sides. Waited.

He'd seen her naked often, yet here, at this moment,

she felt sick with self-consciousness, wanting to cover herself with her hands.

She found herself wondering how, in this blaze of sunlight, she could feel so cold.

His hand moved, gesturing her courteously towards the rug. She walked over and sat down, trying not to curl too obviously into a ball.

The red and white horse was lying beside her, wheels in the air. She picked it up and placed it carefully at a distance. *Oh, Tom...*

She saw Remy reach into the back pocket of his jeans and extract his wallet. For one dreadful moment she thought he was going to offer her money, and braced herself for the shame of it. Then she saw the tiny packet in his hand and realised.

He must have heard her slight indrawn breath, because he looked at her, his mouth twisting. 'This time you have no husband to act as fall-guy,' he told her unsmilingly. 'So we must put safety before passion, hmm?'

Passion? Her dazed brain repeated the word. Is that what this is?

He walked across and knelt beside her. His hand brushed her body, passing lightly from her shoulder, over the tip of one pointed breast and down to her belly. He parted her slender thighs, his fingers questing almost insolently to ascertain her readiness.

He said, with a faint inflection of surprise, 'So, in spite of everything, you want me. *Alors...* '

He did not attempt to undress, merely unzipping his

jeans. Then she was under him, aware that he was adjusting the condom before he entered her without preliminaries—just one swift, deep thrust.

She realised he was not even looking at her as he drove into her, his body moving in its usual easy, fluid rhythm. And she closed her eyes so that she would not have to see him—endure the hurt of him not looking at her.

*Not looking, not smiling, not murmuring. Not loving...*

Nor did he prolong the encounter, his body swiftly almost clinically attaining its climax.

*'Merci.'* His voice was cool as he lifted himself away from her. 'Your body is still an exquisite adventure, Alys. One would never think you had given birth to a child.'

She sat up slowly, numbly, reaching for her robe. Almost unable to comprehend what had just transpired between them. Feeling as if the strong inner core of her had crumbled.

'But I regret that you have humbled yourself in vain,' he went on. 'Your charming acquiescence has made no difference to my plans. I *will* have my son.'

He got to his feet, refastening his jeans, while she huddled the robe round her, aware that her teeth were chattering. As he turned away she scrambled upright too, and ran to him, catching his arm.

'Remy—please.' There was anguish in her voice. 'Oh, God, if you ever loved me...'

He took her hand, detaching it from his sleeve with a kind of terrible finality.

'And what love,' he said softly, 'could possibly survive what you have done to me? Tell me that—if you can.'

He paused, adding flatly, 'My lawyers will contact you, *madame*.'

Standing silent and bereft, she watched him walk away.

Knowing that, this time, it would be for ever.

And unable even to cry.

# CHAPTER ELEVEN

ALLIE poured shower gel into her cupped hand and began to work it into her skin, wondering as she did so if she would ever feel loved again.

She'd been used, but not abused, and whatever violation there'd been was of her heart, not her body.

He'd taken her quickly and casually, as if demonstrating that although she might still appeal to him physically she had no hold over his emotions.

But what else could she expect? Had she really believed that offering herself sexually might change Remy's mind, or soften his attitude towards her?

If so, she'd made a desperate mistake. All that she'd done was make him despise her even more. And, once again, she had no one to blame but herself, she thought wearily.

Except—except that the hand asserting its dominant sweep down her body had seemed to tremble a little. Or was that simply a forlorn hope?

It certainly did nothing to alleviate her sense of shame. Of failure. Or the agony of regret that clawed at her even now. The realisation of all she had lost.

'I should hate him,' she whispered to herself. 'I have every reason in the world to do so. But I can't— I can't… And, God help me, I never shall.'

She rinsed the gel from her body, and the shampoo from her hair, then towelled herself dry, trying to get her thoughts under control. To make some kind of coherent plan for the immediate future.

She could not, of course, tell Tante any of it. She could not distress her like that. Although if Remy carried out his threat to fight for Tom's custody then her great-aunt would have to know, and sooner rather than later.

She sighed unhappily. Well, she thought, sufficient unto the day and all that…

In the meantime, everything had to appear as normal as she could make it. Just as if she'd actually spent a peaceful afternoon playing with Tom without a care in the world.

She put on a pretty blue and white floral skirt in floating georgette, adding a scoop-neck white top. She combed back her still-damp hair, and tucked it behind her ears.

Leaving Tom still asleep, she went down to the garden and collected up the rug and her bikini, bundling it all, together with her robe, into the washing machine housed in an outbuilding. Then she went back for Tom's hat, the sun lotion and the wooden toys. She found the cow and the duck readily enough, but there was no sign of the red and white horse.

It's probably up in his cot, she thought with a shrug

as she walked back into the kitchen. And found herself stopping dead.

Solange Geran was standing in the middle of the room, arms folded across her body, the pretty face distorted by sullen anger.

Allie gave her a level glance as she deposited the things she was carrying on the table.

'*Bonjour, mademoiselle,*' she said with cool politeness. 'I didn't hear you knock.'

'For that there is a reason,' Solange said rudely. 'I did not bother.'

'Madame Colville is not at home.'

'It was not her I came to see.' The other girl took a step nearer, glaring at her. Allie had to fight an impulse to retreat. 'I thought it was you I saw on the road yesterday. I want to know what you think you are doing? Why have you dared to come back here, when you must know you are not wanted?'

'I came to visit my great-aunt,' Allie returned quietly. 'It didn't take much daring.'

*Oh, God, if you knew—if you really knew…*

'But you would not, I hope, be stupid enough to think you could throw yourself at Remy again,' Solange challenged scornfully. 'Because you would be wasting your time. He finished with you long ago.'

Allie looked down at the toys. 'Not—completely, perhaps. There are still—issues…'

'You think Remy welcomes this new tie between you?' Solange almost spat. 'He does not. *C'est une affaire ridicule.*'

He must have gone straight to her, Allie thought numbly. Told her everything. Or perhaps not—everything...

She threw back her head. 'Then why doesn't he simply—walk away?'

'Because he is devoted to his grandfather,' Solange said pettishly. 'Even when the old man is determined to make a fool of himself—and at his age too.' She snorted. 'My mother says it is disgusting.'

'His grandfather?' Allie stared at her. 'What are you talking about?'

Solange shrugged. 'The wedding, *naturellement.*' She paused, her eyes widening. 'You mean you do not know? But perhaps Madame Colville thinks it will be less embarrassing for both families if you do not attend.' She laughed unpleasantly. *'Elle a raison, bien sûr.'*

Allie's mind was reeling. 'You're saying that Tante Madelon is going to *marry* Remy's grandfather? Oh, I don't believe it.'

And yet, she realized, shocked, many of the things that had bewildered her were now beginning to make a horrible kind of sense.

That's why Tante got me here, she thought. So that she could break the news, slowly and kindly. Only she's found it harder than she thought...

'Believe—do not believe.' Solange shrugged again. *'Ça ne fait rien.* Who cares what you think? It will be good when you have returned to England and can trouble us no more.'

'And Remy's against—this marriage?'

'*Certainement.* What else?'

'But Tante's his patient.' Allie shook her head. 'I thought—I had the impression—that they—liked each other.'

'They have a professional relationship.' Solange pursed her lips. 'But he would hardly wish for a relative of *yours* to live at Trehel. *C'est une embêtement.*'

A nuisance was putting it mildly, thought Allie. It sounded like a nightmare waiting to happen. Tante—and Georges de Brizat! It didn't seem possible. Although she knew that in other circumstances she'd have been happy for them. Cheered them on.

'But at least Remy lives in his own house, and we will be able to keep our distance when the time comes,' Solange added with airy dismissal.

Allie's throat tightened. She said quietly, 'I'm sure that will be a relief to my great-aunt too—if the marriage ever happens, of course.'

Solange's eyes narrowed. 'You will try to prevent it?'

'By no means. But—things happen.' And there's a time bomb waiting to explode in this relationship, she thought wretchedly. When Remy makes his intentions public. Would he take this into consideration, or would he see it as something of a bonus—an opportunity to rid himself of a potential embarrassment? Could he be that cruel?

I just don't know any more, she told herself with sadness.

She looked back at Solange. 'I won't be waiting

around for the wedding—if that's the assurance you've come for, *mademoiselle*.'

'I also wish to be sure that you will not contact Remy. That you accept you have nothing to hope for from him.'

'No,' Allie said, after a pause. 'I have no hopes at all. And now I'd like you to go.'

Solange gave her another glare and turned away, but as she did so there was a sleepy wail from upstairs. Tom had woken up.

Solange checked, frowning. 'You have a child? I did not know.'

Allie lifted her chin. 'Perhaps it wasn't considered any of your business, *mademoiselle*.' Although it may concern you sooner than you expect, she thought with sudden anguish. Oh, Remy, what are you doing to me? Of all the women in the world to be Tom's stepmother...

She mastered herself with an effort. Looked the other girl calmly in the eye. 'Please close the door behind you.'

She waited for the pick-up to drive off before she flew upstairs, where Tom was crying properly now— cross, red-faced, in tears as he shook the bars of his cot. She lifted him out, holding him to her so tightly that he struggled in protest.

Allie talked to him soothingly as she changed him then dressed him in shorts and tee-shirt, coaxing him out of his bad mood.

'Did you have a bad dream, my love?' she whispered. 'Because I feel as if I'm living through the worst possible one. But I can't let myself cry—not yet. I don't think I can even afford to be scared.'

She'd regained some of her composure and Tom was in his highchair, dealing with a beaker of milk, when Tante returned, her silver hair swept into an elegant swirl on top of her head.

'Very chic,' Allie approved. She paused, forcing an approximation of a teasing smile. 'Is that how you're going to wear it for your wedding?'

'You know?' Tante's expression of dismay was almost comical. 'But how?'

Allie looked back, deliberately expressionless. 'I had a visit from an old friend—Mademoiselle Geran.'

'That one!' Tante's tone was outraged. 'With her finger in every pie. What was *she* doing here?'

'She came to—warn me off.'

*'Mon Dieu.'* Tante took a sharp breath. 'What insolence.'

'Clearly she thinks she has the right.' Allie managed a shrug. 'She wishes me to vanish, never to return, and maybe in her shoes I'd feel the same.'

Tante snorted delicately. 'Perhaps her pursuit of Remy has not been as successful as she first hoped.'

Allie's gaze sharpened. 'You implied they were going to be married.'

'That has certainly always been her intention,' Tante said drily. 'And his father favours the match because he wishes to see him settled, and therefore unlikely to go on his travels again. *Alors*, with Remy himself one can never be sure.' She pursed her lips. 'But sometimes all that is needed is persistence, and Solange Geran is a pretty girl, who wants him, which is always flattering.'

She paused, her eyes reflective as she studied her great-niece's pale face. 'Besides, *ma chère*, he is young and very much a man, and it must be lonely for him at Trehel in that house he created for love.'

'Don't.' Allie's voice broke. 'Oh, please, don't…'

She turned away, burying her face in her hands, and *madame* moved to her, putting her arms round the slender shaking figure and soothing her quietly.

'Go to him, *ma chère*,' she urged. 'Tell him how you feel. What have you to lose?'

Allie shook her head. 'I—can't. It—it's much too late for that.' *And I've lost already—disastrously.*

'I should not have brought you back here,' Madelon Colville said with a sigh. 'Except that I thought— both Georges and I hoped—' She broke off, shaking her head. 'But one should never interfere.'

Allie lifted her chin, a smile nailed in place. 'Let's talk about something else, shall we? Your good news? How did it all happen?'

'We knew each other from childhood. Georges says that I was his first love.' *Madame's* half-shrug was deliciously cynical. 'But I was certainly not his last. We happened to meet one day—after Remy had gone away—and we talked a little. The next time we talked more, and our meetings began to be arranged. *Et—voilà.*'

She shook her head. 'It was not what we had ever expected, you understand. And there are many who would say we are too old. But love is good whenever it is found. And I am happy again in a way I did not dream was possible. But I am angry that Solange should have come here to make mischief,' she added roundly. 'She must know that I wished to tell you myself.'

'I wish you had.'

'I wish it also. But I too was waiting only for the right moment, and once again it has gone wrong.' She sighed again. 'It has not been—easy, you understand. For Georges or myself. Remy's father took his departure very badly.'

Allie bit her lip. No one, she thought, had to tell her that. She said stiltedly, 'You shouldn't be blamed for my sins.'

'Mine too,' Tante said gently. 'I could have spoken, *chérie*. But I did not.'

Tom interrupted at this point, demanding vociferously to get down from his chair, his eyes fixed on his toys, still on the table.

'Here, darling.' Allie put them on the floor . 'But I don't know what you've done with your horse—unless you've eaten it.'

It was good to watch him playing, see him look up and laugh. But while she smiled, and clapped her hands, Allie was thinking hard.

Somehow she was going to have to talk to Remy, she realised with disquiet. Try and make him see that this marriage deserved a chance, persuade him to do some kind of deal.

Even if he hates me, he must love his grandfather and want his happiness, she told herself.

And I must do this for Tante's sake—no matter what the cost may be.

She shivered.

It was market day in Ignac, and Allie threaded the baby buggy carefully through the crowds thronging round the stalls as she crossed the square towards the medical centre.

She'd bought extra tee-shirts for Tom, which had been her excuse for the trip.

Now she had to fulfil the real purpose of the exercise.

She hoped she'd got her timing right. She'd found a leaflet with instructions about surgery hours, and figured that Remy would have dealt with his morning patients and be about to start on his visits. So she made her way to the small car park at the rear of the building and waited.

Ten minutes later he appeared, striding through the glass doors, his medical case in one hand, turning to call something over his shoulder as he emerged.

Swallowing, Allie moved forward to intercept him. 'Remy—can we talk?'

He checked instantly, his brows snapping together as he looked down at Tom. 'Is the baby sick?'

'No, he's fine. But there's something I need to say—to ask you.'

'And you chose here?' He glanced around him, his mouth twisting. 'You would not prefer to find somewhere more private, where your powers of persuasion might have—more scope?'

'No,' she said, steadily. 'I don't think so.'

'A pity,' Remy drawled insolently. 'I enjoyed the reminder of how delightful you are naked.'

She felt her face warm. Had to force herself to stand her ground, as the blue eyes moved down her body, mentally stripping her, she realised, all over again. And quite deliberately.

She said, 'I learned yesterday that Tante Madelon is to marry your grandfather.'

He shrugged. 'It seems so,' he countered brusquely. 'What of it?'

'This is a good time for them—a happy time. I wouldn't want anything to spoil that.'

'Ah,' he said softly. 'I begin to see. You think to appeal to my sentimental side, *ma belle. Pas de chance.*'

He walked past her, using the remote control to unlock his car.

'Remy—listen—please.' She turned desperately. 'They've—found each other. After all these years. They want to spend the time they have left together.'

'And your point is?'

'If there's a court case over Tom it will force them to take sides. It could ruin their hopes for the future.' She took a step nearer. 'Isn't punishing me enough for you? Do they have to suffer too? Please think about what you're doing before it's too late.'

His laugh was harsh. 'Since when, *madame*, have you cared so much for the feelings—the happiness—of other people?'

Her chin lifted in challenge. 'And since when have *you* cared so little—Dr de Brizat?' She paused. 'If you—leave Tom with me, I swear that you'll still see him. As often as I can arrange. Once Tante and your grandfather are married, no one will think it strange if I visit Trehel.'

His brows lifted. 'Occasional visits?' he questioned jeeringly. 'More pretence? I don't think so. But there does not have to be a court case. You may, if you wish, voluntarily grant me custody of my son. A private matter between us, with no vulgar publicity. I might even allow you to visit him sometimes—if I am offered sufficient inducement,' he added softly.

There was a silence, then Allie said bitterly, 'I would never have believed you could be so cruel.'

His smile was hard. 'Everything I know, I learned from you, *ma belle*.' He glanced at his watch. 'I must go. Let me know if you wish to—negotiate terms.' He walked across and bent over the buggy, kissing the top of Tom's head. '*Au revoir, mon brave.*' He straightened, his eyes meeting hers. 'When you have a moment, you might teach him to say Papa,' he told her mockingly. '*A bientôt, Alys.*'

She stood gripping the handle of the buggy, watching him drive away.

That did no good at all, she thought wretchedly. In fact I've probably made things a damned sight worse.

She began to make her way back to where her own car was parked, so lost in her unhappy thoughts that she never noticed the figure standing motionless in the shade of the building. Or realised that Solange Geran's gaze was following her like a dark, malignant shadow in the sun.

'Are you really returning to England at the weekend?' Tante asked sadly. 'Can I not persuade you to stay for a little longer? Thomas so loves it here,' she added persuasively. 'He is a different child since he came. He is walking well, and he talks all the time—although it is not always certain what he is saying, of course. And he laughs and plays, and is not shy with anyone.'

'He's been transformed,' Allie admitted, her eyes travelling to her son, who was chasing a butterfly between intervals of falling over amid squeals of delight. 'And it's wonderful. But—the ferry's all booked.'

She leaned back in her chair, a hand shading her eyes from the sun dappling through the leaves of the tree. 'Besides, it would be better if I went as planned. I feel that, at the very least, I—I'm something of an embarrassment.'

'But there is so much still to be resolved,' her great-aunt protested. 'How can you leave—feeling as you do for Remy—and not tell him?'

'Because it wouldn't be something he wants to hear,' Allie said tonelessly. 'Too much has happened that he can't possibly forgive.'

Tante looked at her gravely. 'But you have given him

a child, Alys.' She saw Allie's eyes widen in shock, and nodded. 'Let us now speak openly, *ma mie*, and forget this myth that Thomas is a child of the Marchingtons. One has only to look at him to know the truth. Ask Madame Drouac, if you do not believe me,' she added drily. 'And Remy has a right to know this.'

Allie bent her head. She said in a low voice, 'He knows already. He came here unexpectedly a few days ago and—saw Tom.'

Tante gasped. 'Remy was here?' Her voice was incredulous. 'But why?'

'I don't know. He simply—arrived.'

'*Mon Dieu*. And you said nothing?'

'I didn't know how to tell you.' Allie shuddered. 'It was a nightmare. We—quarrelled terribly, because I'd kept the baby's existence from him along with everything else, and now he hates me more than ever.' She closed her eyes. 'In fact he's so angry he's threatening to take Tom away from me. Assume sole custody.'

There was a horrified silence, then, 'No—and no,' Tante declared strongly. 'I do not believe it. I cannot. To part a young child and his mother? Remy would not do such a thing.'

Allie's smile was bitter. 'Maybe he thinks I'm not fit to be Tom's mother.' She sighed. 'He's changed—and I'm afraid that's my fault.'

'Not in his heart, *chérie*.' Madame's voice gentled. 'That is impossible.' She paused. 'Remy has the de Brizat temper, but, like a summer storm, it is soon over. Once he is over the shock of knowing he has a son, he will listen to reason. Agree to—some compromise. I am certain of it.'

Allie shrugged unhappily. 'All the same, I'm just waiting to hear from his lawyer,' she said. 'Expecting the axe to fall, but not knowing exactly when.' She bit her lip. 'I thought that if I wasn't around, if I went back to England, he might become a little less angry, perhaps.'

She took a deep breath. 'And, of course, somehow I have to break the news to Lady Marchington. God knows what *her* reaction will be.'

Tante looked austere. 'It can hardly be any surprise to her. She must have known the truth would emerge one day.'

'No,' Allie said. 'I—don't think she ever did. She wanted Hugo's son to carry on the Marchington name—and together they invented this fantasy that Tom was Hugo's child. Only for Grace it's become a reality, and she'll fight to keep it. In fact, I dread to think what she might do.'

She sighed again. 'Oh, God, what a mess I've made of everything.'

Tante patted her hand. 'It has not been completely of your making, *chérie*. That marriage of yours—a disaster. If your father had lived, he would never have permitted it. Never! But your mother—all she could see was the title, the money, and the grand estate. Nothing else concerned her.'

And all I could see, Allie thought sadly, was a man in a wheelchair who said he needed me. Whose very survival seemed to be somehow my responsibility. So I put on my idealist's hat and walked into the trap.

'I should have stood up to them when I knew I was pregnant,' she said slowly. 'Instead of going along with this—madness. I should have walked out there and then. Made my own life.'

'Perhaps. Yet it is not so easy when there is a child to consider. It is a woman's instinct to protect, I think. To do what is necessary for the well-being of her baby, even if there has to be sacrifice.'

Sacrifice, Allie thought with a shudder. That's a terrible word.

Tom came trotting over to present her with a handful of grass and a pebble. She admired them and thanked him for them with due solemnity, and was rewarded by his father's slanting smile before he toddled off.

She watched him go, her heart twisting uncontrollably.

I've lost the only man I ever loved, she thought. If I lose my baby as well, what will I do? How can I live if I have nothing? *Nothing?*

And prayed that she would never have to find out.

## CHAPTER TWELVE

A DAY passed, and then another, but there was still no word from Remy. No communication from a lawyer. No request for Tom to be subjected to any form of test.

This is what it must be like to be standing in the dock, thought Allie. Waiting for the judge to pass sentence. Knowing that no plea of mitigation—no appeal—is going to make the slightest difference.

'I feel as if I'm living on a knife-edge,' she told Tante restlessly. 'I can only suppose he's biding his time. Waiting until I get back to England. I don't know what the legal procedure is in cases like this.'

She paused. 'Does anyone at Trehel know what he's planning? Has—has anything been said?'

'Not one word.' Tante shook her head. 'And if Georges knew, he would have told me.' Her face was strained. 'After all, Thomas is his great-grandson. He could not have kept such a thing to himself.'

Allie bit her lip. 'When he finds out—will it make trouble between you? Because that's the last thing I want.'

Tante sighed. 'That, *mon enfant*, is in the lap of the

gods. But life must go on,' she added briskly. 'And I have business in Ignac. Do you wish to come with me?'

Allie shook her head. 'Tom's in a scratchy mood. I think he's cutting another tooth.' Or maybe he's picking up on my tensions, she thought. If I just knew what I was up against. If only something—anything would happen...

But there was nothing like coping with a fractious toddler for taking your mind off your problems, she thought a couple of hours later, when Tom had finally fallen asleep on her lap after a heavy-duty session with his favourite nursery rhyme book.

She'd sung the old verses to him over and over again until she was practically hoarse, letting her voice sink lower as his eyelids drooped.

She eased him gently into the corner of the sofa and got up, stretching, to make herself some coffee. She was waiting for the kettle to boil when the telephone sounded shrilly.

'Wake Tom, whoever you are, and I'll kill you,' she muttered under her breath as she flew to answer it.

'Alice, is that you?'

She'd almost forgotten how icily autocratic Grace Marchington could sound—even at a distance. And this was a reminder she certainly hadn't bargained for.

She said slowly, 'Lady Marchington—this is a surprise. Is there something I can do for you?'

'Yes,' Grace Marchington said. 'I'd like you to bring my grandson home where he belongs. At once.'

'I'm afraid I'm not prepared to do that,' Allie

returned. 'We'll be returning at the weekend, as arranged.'

'But it should be perfectly possible to book an earlier crossing—this evening or early tomorrow—and I require you to do that.'

Alice took a deep breath. 'Lady Marchington, you seem to have forgotten I came to spend some time with my great-aunt.'

'Ah, yes.' There was sudden venom in the other woman's tone. 'The famous sick woman who has, in fact, nothing wrong with her at all. Quite the contrary, I'm told. I suppose this was a scheme you cooked up together—to get Thomas away from me? Well, it won't work. You are to bring him back immediately, Alice. After which I shall consider your position very carefully. So be warned. The child belongs here—with me.'

Allie stiffened. The point of no return, she thought, had finally been reached.

'No,' she said quietly. 'He doesn't. And you know that as well as I do. I should also warn you that his real father knows it too, and intends to sue for custody.'

There was a silence. Then, 'My dear Alice,' said Grace Marchington. She sounded almost amused. 'You have either been drinking or had too much sun, because you are clearly delusional. My beloved Hugo was Thomas's father. And that is the end of the matter.'

'No,' Alice said strongly. 'It's just the beginning. And all this pretending has to stop. You have to see that. Remy wants his child, and he'll do whatever it takes to get him.'

'Remy?' the older woman said slowly. 'I suppose you're referring to that wild-eyed young Frenchman who appeared here one morning after your last ill-advised trip to Brittany, demanding to see you. Claiming he wished you to accompany him to—Brazil, perhaps? I did not pay much attention.'

'Remy came to Marchington Hall?' For a moment Allie felt as if her heart had stopped beating. 'And you sent him away—without letting him speak to me?'

'Naturally. You were my son's wife. I told him that you were not there. That you had confessed everything to Hugo and been forgiven, and that you had both gone away for a few days. A second honeymoon to enable you to put an—essentially trivial piece of foolishness behind you.'

She paused. 'I may even have hinted that it was not the first time you had—strayed, but that in the end you would never seriously jeopardise your comfortable lifestyle in England. That you would always know which side your bread was buttered.'

She gave a light laugh. 'A vulgarity, but he seemed to understand what I meant, and left without further protest.'

'Oh, dear God.' Allie's voice was hushed with shock. 'He came for me, and you told him—all that?'

'I would have done more,' said Lady Marchington. 'To prevent our family name being tarnished by a slut like you. And you have not changed. Because now, it seems, you are using my grandchild in a pathetic attempt to get your former lover back. Using any lie, any subterfuge, to rekindle your *affaire* with him—just as she said.'

'*She* said?' Allie repeated. 'What are you talking about? Who is *she*?'

'I had a hysterical phone call from a young woman—a Mademoiselle Geran. It appears she once read some magazine article about your wedding to Hugo, and remembered our name. Traced me because of it,' she added with distaste.

'Solange?' Allie found she was fighting for breath. 'Oh, God—I don't believe it.'

'I suppose I should be grateful to her. She said you were pursuing this man—throwing yourself at him—although she was on the point of getting engaged to him herself. She told me that she had seen you together, and she was convinced you were trying to make him believe Thomas might be his by pretending that some—superficial resemblance meant more than it did. She thinks you should be stopped. And I, my dear Alice, tend to agree with her.'

Alice felt sick. She said curtly, 'I can't speak for Mademoiselle Geran's relationship with Remy, but there's no question of my being reconciled with him. Quite the opposite, in fact. And he saw Tom completely by accident and drew his own conclusions, so she's wrong about that too.'

'But you—you stupid little bitch—you told him the truth?' Grace's voice was a menacing snarl.

'Grace—modern science will provide him with all

the proof he needs.' Allie spoke wearily. 'Denial was totally pointless. And, anyway, I wasn't prepared to lie to him. Not now, or in the future when—if—it goes to court.'

'Thomas is my grandson.' The older woman's voice rose furiously. 'A Marchington, and the last of his name. I will admit nothing different, and I will *not* allow this Frenchman to have him. Now, you will bring the boy back to England within twenty-four hours. Do I make myself clear?'

'As crystal,' Allie flung back at her. 'But it doesn't change a thing. Tom is my child, and Remy's his natural father. And, the way things are, I stand to lose him too. So I'm fighting for myself here, Grace. Not an inheritance to which my son isn't entitled, and which doesn't really matter a damn.'

She paused. 'No doubt the lawyers will be able to come up with some long-forgotten distant cousin to take his place, and you'll just have to bite the bullet and retire. You've played and lost, Grace, and you have to accept it. My only regret is that I ever let you do it. I must have been crazy.'

And she replaced the receiver and stood for a while, staring into space, her arms wrapped tightly round her body.

So, she thought, it's all out in the open at last—and that has to be totally the right thing. So why am I feeling more scared now than I've ever been before?

And she shivered.

* * *

'I've decided to go back to England, but not to Marchington Hall,' Allie said quietly as she and Tante sat together that evening. 'That's quite impossible. There's no point in turning to my mother either, so I'll try and find somewhere cheap, look for a day nursery for Tom, and get a job before what money I have runs out.' She forced a smile. 'I'm sure Grace will already have taken steps to cancel my allowance from the estate.'

She added with difficulty, 'If you could just make it clear to Remy that I'm—not running away or hiding. Just trying to get my life in order. And that as soon as I have a permanent address you'll pass it on to him, so that things can be settled—one way or the other.'

'No, Alys.' Tante's voice was anguished. 'I cannot let you do this. Remy would never wish it, I know. You must stay here, so that you can meet with him and talk calmly. Decide what is best for your child. That is the only way.'

'I don't think Remy and I can do calm.' Allie tried to speak lightly. 'Too much has happened. But perhaps if I'm not around, and he has time to think—to weigh up everything involved—perhaps there could be— some kind of compromise.'

She shook her head. 'Otherwise it means a court case, scandal and tabloid headlines. All the sordid details. And I don't want that kind of stigma attached to my son. Because he won't be a baby for ever, and one day he'll know. And I—I couldn't bear that.'

'It will not come to that,' Madame Colville said fiercely. 'It cannot.'

'That,' Allie said sadly, 'is what I'm trying very hard to believe.'

She was restless the next day, unable to settle to anything, her mind in turmoil. And Tom was in full grizzling mode over the new tooth, one reddened cheek advertising his discomfort.

Between us, we're the pair from hell, Allie thought wryly.

'I think I'll drive into Ignac,' she announced. 'Go to the pharmacy before it closes, and see if they can recommend something for him.'

And maybe, she thought, give it one last shot with Remy before she departed for England.

It took all the nerve she possessed to walk into the medical centre and ask for him. But she was to be disappointed. The receptionist told her that Dr de Brizat had left for the day, and asked if she wished for an appointment for the following morning.

Allie thanked her, but refused.

I shall be packing tomorrow, she thought. And perhaps this wasn't such a good idea anyway.

She applied some of the teething remedy to Tom's sore gum, and gave him a spoonful of the pink medicine that had also been suggested, and he fell asleep halfway back to Les Sables.

About half a mile from the house, she saw a car parked on the verge, and realised that someone had stepped into the road and was waving frantically at her. To her astonishment, she saw it was Madame Drouac.

She pulled over and opened the window. 'What's the matter,' she gasped in French. 'Is it *madame*? Has something happened?'

*'Non, non,'* the other woman assured her. She pushed a folded sheet of paper into Allie's hand. *'Lisez, madame."*

It had begun, Allie saw, as a shopping list, then abruptly changed.

Do not come to the house. Your mother-in-law is here, with a woman she claims is a psychiatric nurse. She says you are suffering a breakdown caused by postnatal depression and grief for your late husband, and she is here to take charge of Thomas. I am afraid for you, my child, and for your little son. Go to the Hotel du Parc in Ignac and I will contact you there when it is safe.

'Oh, dear God,' Allie whispered. She looked numbly at Madame Drouac. 'Will you go back to *madame*? Make sure she's safe.'

A warm, capable hand descended on her shoulder and patted it. *'Allez, madame. Allez vite.'*

Allie turned the car and set off. But after she'd gone about a mile she pulled into the side of the road and stopped. She was shaking and nauseous, her mind reeling.

She smoothed the crumpled paper and read it again.

Grace is mad, she thought. Completely mad. She has to be—to imagine she can get away with something like this.

Yet why shouldn't she? said a voice in her head. You were ill after Tom was born, so the medical evidence is there. And she's already discussed your 'problems' with Dr Lennard. Therefore, what's to prevent you being whisked into some convenient nursing home and kept there, under sedation if necessary, while she does as she wishes with Tom?

And somehow she'll make bloody sure that Remy never sees him again—even if she has to take him to the other side of the world.

While I—I'll have just—disappeared.

She shook her head. Oh, come on, she adjured herself. This is conspiracy theory gone berserk. People don't behave like this. Grace couldn't. She wouldn't...

She stopped. Forced herself to consider. To remember. Grace and Hugo, she thought. Hugo and Grace. Both single-minded, both suffering from tunnel vision where the Marchington name and inheritance were concerned. At what point, she wondered, did obsession tip over into something even darker? A place where ordinary rules no longer applied?

Had there always been some flaw—some genetic kink—that made them feel they were somehow immune from the demands of normal conduct? Had she secretly suspected this all along—which was why she'd originally decided not to marry Hugo? Because there was always—something?

Thank God Tom isn't his child, she thought. Thank God he belongs to Remy, who may have a temper, but who's also decent and dedicated, tough and vulnerable, passionate and gentle. And who once loved me so much more than I deserved.

And who would now love his son and protect him always. If he had the chance.

Allie raised her head, gazing sightlessly ahead of her through the windscreen.

Grace will find me, she thought. She only has to tell the police that I'm mentally incapable and I have a child with me, and they're bound to start searching. I thought I could deal with her. But that was before I realised the lengths she might go to.

I don't care what she does to me, but I have to stop her taking Tom. Destroying his innocence and his pleasure in life for her own twisted purpose. I have to find somewhere safe for him that she can't reach.

And I know now where I must turn. Because I realise that there's only ever been one place—one person.

What was it Tante had said? That a woman with a child had to do what was necessary, even if there had to be sacrifice?

The tears were hot and thick in her throat, but she choked them back. There was no time to cry now. She would weep afterwards. After she had done what she had to do. What was necessary.

She started the car and drove to Trehel.

Tom was still asleep when she got there, so she left the car quietly and walked to the door alone.

They said in Ignac that you'd gone home, she whispered silently. So be here. Please be here.

She knocked and waited. Then the door opened and he was standing there, the dark brows snapping into a frown.

'Alys?' There was a note of incredulity in his tone. 'What are you doing here?'

He was wearing close-fitting charcoal pants, and his white shirt hung open over them. His bare feet were thrust into espadrilles, and his hair was still damp from the shower. Her aching senses picked up the tormenting fragrance of soap and warm clean skin. Taunted her with them.

'I—I had to see you.' She hesitated. 'But I seem to have picked a bad time. Are you going out?'

'Later.'

'With Solange?' The question was uttered before she could stop herself.

Remy propped a shoulder against the door frame. 'No,' he said. 'There is a card game tonight at the Café des Sports.' His mouth twisted. 'Does that satisfy your curiosity?'

Her face was burning. 'I—I'm sorry,' she mumbled. 'It—it's none of my business.'

'No,' he said with a touch of bleakness. 'It is not.' He paused. 'What do you want with me, Alys? Why are you here?'

She stared at him across the abyss of her own making. The great pit of misunderstanding and bitterness that seemed to be widening—deepening between them with every moment that passed. Somehow she had to reach out to him. Not for her own sake—she had already forfeited all chance of that. But for Tom, who was precious to them both. For Tom…

Her voice was a stranger's, small and strained. 'I came to say that I—I'm giving you the baby.'

Once the impossible, the agonising words had been spoken, others came, in an urgent, stumbling rush.

'I've brought him to you. Our child—our little son. I want you to take him for me. To love him and keep him safe. Because I realise that you're the only one who can.'

'In the name of God,' he said. 'What are you saying?'

'I'm telling you I've changed my mind. Because we can't fight over him, Remy. It's—wrong. He's part of you—part of me. We'd just be tearing ourselves in pieces.'

'Alys,' he said. 'Listen…'

'No, you listen—please. He'll have a good life with you. I know that. This is a wonderful place to grow up in. He won't be imprisoned here—or warped—or any of the things I dread might happen to him if I'm not around to protect him.'

She swallowed, her hands clenching into fists at her sides, her nails scoring her palms. 'If you—take him, I—I won't interfere. I promise. I won't be a nuisance, or make any demands. He'll be yours. But you said—once—that you'd let me see him sometimes.'

She spread her hands in a gesture of supplication. Of surrender. 'So you can impose any conditions you like. I—I'll do whatever you want—be whatever you

want—if—if that's how it must be… But please—
dear God—please let me come here occasionally—so
he doesn't forget me.'

Her voice cracked, and with it the last remnants of
her control. The tears she'd tried to dam back were
suddenly smothering her. Crushing her. And she sank
under their weight down to the ground at his feet and
knelt there, her whole body shaking under the force
of her sobbing.

Dimly, she heard him swear, softly and succinctly.
Then she found herself being raised, lifted into his
arms, and carried into the house.

A sofa received her, and she shrank into its softness,
an arm hiding her blurred and swollen eyes. She was
aware of him moving about. The chink of glass. Then
a bunch of tissues being pushed into her hand and a
tumbler held to her lips.

She winced away from the smell of spirits. 'What
is it?' Her voice was drowned and shaking.

'Whisky,' he said. 'Drink it.'

She obeyed, choking a little. Felt warmth begin to
penetrate the Arctic night within her.

Eventually, she dared to look at him. He was seated
at the other end of the sofa, his own glass clasped
between his hands as he gazed down at the floor.

He said quietly, 'You say you have—brought our
child to me? Without warning—or discussion? But
how could you do such a thing. And why?'

Mutely, she fumbled in the pocket of her skirt and
passed him Tante's warning note. She saw him read

it, then go back to the beginning and examine it again, his sudden frown deepening thunderously.

'How did you get this?'

She said tonelessly, 'Madame Drouac was waiting for me on the road. Tante Madelon must have pretended she was sending her shopping.'

She swallowed. 'My mother-in-law is a very plausible, very powerful woman. The family doctor in England is totally under her thumb, and I know she's already put the idea into his head that I need therapy. I—I didn't take it seriously at the time, but I do now. I also realise I'd have a problem protecting Tom from her in England. That she wouldn't hesitate to use him as leverage against me if necessary.

'So, I—turned around and came here. You see, I was desperate. I didn't know what else to do.'

'Ah,' Remy said quietly. *'Oui, je comprends.'* He downed his whisky in one swift movement and rose to his feet. 'You have left Thomas in the car?'

She nodded. 'He's asleep. He's been teething. I bought some stuff from the pharmacy. But I thought, as you're a doctor, you'll know what's best to do for him.'

'Will I?' His smile did not reach his eyes. 'I hope you are right.' He walked to the door and disappeared outside.

As Allie turned to put her glass on a table beside the sofa, her hand brushed something that moved, and she realised she was holding a little red and white horse on wheels. She stared at it for a long moment, then gently put it back where she'd found it.

It was some time before Remy returned, and he was alone.

Allie reared up in alarm. 'Where is he? Oh, God—has something happened?'

'He is at the house,' he said. 'Being worshipped by my father and grandfather. Also by Madame Lastaine.' His mouth twisted. 'He will need to be rescued before she attempts to feed him.'

She sank back against the cushions. 'I thought for one awful moment that Grace might have found him.' She shook her head. 'I'm still scared that she'll find a way of taking Tom from me and keeping him.'

'But Thomas is with me now,' he said. 'So that cannot happen.' He paused. 'It does not concern you that I might do the same?'

'Yes.' She did not look at him. 'But I have to risk that. Because Tom's safety and happiness are all that matters.'

His head lifted sharply. 'All?'

'All that can be allowed to matter, anyway.' She got to her feet, still clutching the damp ball of tissues. 'And now I'd better go back to Les Sables and face her. Convince her to give it all up as a bad job.'

'An excellent notion. But not yet,' Remy said. 'Now we need to talk. So sit down, Alys.'

She complied reluctantly. 'My great-aunt…'

'My grandfather has telephoned Madame Madelon, and all is well. But she has agreed to spend the night here at Trehel, and bring your clothes and those of Thomas.'

'Oh?' she said. 'And—Lady Marchington?'

'Your mother-in-law was at last persuaded to leave,

on the grounds that guests were expected, but she intends to return tomorrow at ten o'clock. At which time we shall confront her together, you and I. Mother and father.' He paused. 'And husband and wife.'

She said swiftly, 'But we're not—husband and wife.'

'There is the matter of a ceremony,' Remy agreed. 'But that is no great obstacle. And a child should have two parents, don't you think?'

'And so he will,' she said. 'But we certainly don't have to—live under the same roof.' She added hastily, 'If that's what you're suggesting.'

'You asked me if I would let you see Thomas.' He shrugged. 'If you stay, you can see him every day, and probably several times during the night also.'

She bit her lip. 'I—can't do that.' *I can't live in this house where we were so happy together. Not without love—or passion or tenderness. I can't lie beside you at night and know that I'm just—a convenient body. Because it would kill me.*

*I'm not just Tom's mother—I'm the woman who adores and needs you—and I won't settle for some sterile limbo of an existence. It would turn me into some kind of shadow person, and that's no good for Tom either.*

*I don't want him to grow up knowing that I'm simply—tolerated for his sake.*

'No?' He did not sound particularly concerned. 'You have some other plan?'

'Naturally.' She forced an insanely bright note into her voice. 'I have to go back to England and look for a job, somewhere to live. Start to make a—a new life for myself. That—was the original deal, I think.'

'But circumstances change.' Remy paused. 'The Marchington woman—you are not afraid she will seek to be revenged on you in some way?'

'She's going to have her own troubles,' she said. 'Anyway, knowing that I'm homeless and penniless will probably be enough to satisfy her.'

'And that is the life you would choose rather than be married to me?' He sounded politely interested.

'Yes,' Allie said baldly. *Because it won't be as hard or as lonely as living here on sufferance. Wanting you, but having to guard every word—every look.*

'A pity,' he said. 'It means I will have to find a nanny for Thomas. Do you wish to help with the choice of a suitable candidate?'

'No,' she said, smarting under the pain of his careless words. 'Thank you. I'm sure you'll choose the right person.'

'So,' Remy said softly. 'You trust me in something at last.'

Anguish clawed at her. She said with difficulty, 'Don't—please. For Tom's sake we have to put everything that happened behind us. Try to forget.'

'And you can do this?' Remy's voice was suddenly raw. 'I congratulate you, *madame*. Because I am not so fortunate. I, *tu comprends*, I cannot forget. It is not possible.' He drew a harsh breath. 'When I opened the door earlier, and saw you, for one moment I allowed myself to hope that you had come to me.

That you wanted me. But I was wrong. You spoke only of Thomas.'

He shook his head. 'How could you—ask me to take our child without you? Do you truly think so little of me? Am I really such a monster? Do you think I can live only seeing you—sometimes? And that just for the sake of our baby?'

His voice rose. '*Mon Dieu*, Alys, how many more times are you going to break my heart?'

She stared at him, feeling hope tremble into life inside her, but hardly daring to believe it. 'You—love me?'

'Always—always.' He moved, sitting beside her, taking her hands in his and holding them tightly. He said, 'When I reached Paris two years ago, I was hurt and bitter, but I already knew that leaving you was a terrible mistake. That, in spite of everything, you were the only girl I would ever love, and that I should go back, and make you see this. Fight for you, whatever the cost.'

'You followed me to England,' she whispered. '*She* told me that—and what she'd said to you. Second honeymoon! I was probably upstairs—throwing up.'

'Ah, *mon ange*. But I did not know what to believe. It seemed that maybe you had been making a fool of me after all, and that I should go, try to put you out of my mind for ever.'

He raised her hands to his lips, kissing them reverently. 'But I could not. You were there in my mind—in my heart—wherever I went, whatever I did. I could not escape the memory of what we had shared. I also had a dream, Alys, of you as my wife, and the mother of my children. A life together here in this house. As that seemed impossible, I thought—Stop running. Go back and make another life.'

She looked down. 'With Solange?'

'What are you saying? Are you mad?' Incredulity mixed with horror in his voice. 'You think I would involve myself with the woman who gloated over the destruction of our happiness? I swear to you that I have never given her a moment's encouragement.'

'But she thinks—'

'Then that is her problem,' he said. 'Not ours. Because this house held only memories of you.'

'Yet when we met you didn't seem very pleased to see me.'

Remy groaned. 'I was terrified. Because it had occurred to me that your life could have changed so completely that there was no longer any place in it for me.' His smile was wry. 'When you exist for so long on a thread of hope, Alys, you have no wish to see it broken.

'And then, as I feared, you told me that it was over. And I—I reacted badly. I make no excuse for that. But I could not sleep that night for thinking of the touch of your lips, the sweetness of your body in my arms. And I knew I could not—just give up. That I had to try once more to get you back.

'When I came to Les Sables the next day, it was to tell you that I loved you and ask you to be my wife. Then I saw Thomas, and it was as if you had taken all that I felt for you and thrown it back in my face. I felt you must hate me very much if you could have borne my child and not told me.

'And just for a moment I wanted to take him away from you. To destroy your happiness as you had destroyed mine. But when I heard him call you Maman I realised that, although I might threaten, I would never do it. I could not.'

'Is that why you took his toy—the little horse?' Allie asked gently.

'Yes,' he said. 'A gift that you had touched. That he had played with and loved. A small part of something I thought I would have no share in.

'But I still wanted to punish you for trying to hide Thomas from me. I thought if I treated you with equal contempt it would be no more than you deserved.' His mouth curved ruefully. 'But I did not expect my bluff to be called—never believed that you would offer yourself as you did.

'I kept telling myself— She will not go through with this. She cannot. At any moment, she will stop. But you did not. And then—I—could not…'

'But you were so cold,' Allie whispered. 'So—businesslike.'

'I wanted you too badly,' he said frankly. 'I was near the edge—scared of what I might do. I told myself I could not afford to lose control in case I hurt you.' He looked at her remorsefully. 'And I did hurt you, *mon amour*, but in a different way.'

'Did you?' Her eyes were shining, her face transfigured by love. 'I—really can't remember.' She paused. 'But I did try and tell you I was pregnant. Truly.'

'Yes,' he said. 'So you said, and so my father confirmed that night. I had to confide in someone about Thomas or go mad, and we have always been close. But when he heard me speaking so bitterly he said that perhaps I was unjust. That you had once telephoned here, begging to talk to me, and maybe that was what you had wanted to say. Only he had refused to listen, or help. And that if he had been more understanding our lives could have been so different.'

'He was trying to protect you,' she said gently. 'Just as I knew you would always protect your son. And why I could trust you with the rest of his life.'

'And will you trust me with yours?' he asked quietly. *'Mon ange—mon coeur.'*

'Yes,' she said. 'If you still want me. Oh, Remy—Remy.'

Then she was in his arms and his lips were on hers, and they were murmuring brokenly to each other between kisses.

Allie wanted the consummation of their love. She wanted to sink down with him to the rug and offer the surrender of her body for his adoration. But Remy was drawing back with a faint groan.

'We cannot, *mon amour*,' he told her breathlessly. 'Thomas may be getting fretful after all this time. Also, I promised Liliane that I would get my old cot from the attic so that she can clean it for him to sleep in. And my grandfather thinks it would not be *conve-*

*nable* for Madame Madelon to sleep over at the house before they are married, so she must stay here, and her room needs to be prepared.' He looked at her, his mouth rueful, his eyes brimming with sudden laughter. 'Welcome to family life, *ma belle*.'

'It has a nice ring about it,' Allie said, her own lips twitching. 'So we shall just have to wait until tonight, my darling.'

He took her hand. Kissed it. 'Last time, to my eternal shame,' he said quietly, 'I took and gave nothing. Tonight it will be very different. So, will you forgive me, Alys, and lie with me in our bed?'

'Yes,' she told him huskily. 'Oh, yes.' She looked at him from under her lashes, a world of promise shining in her eyes. 'Although poor Tom is teething, remember?' she murmured. 'We could be—disturbed.'

Remy kissed her again, his lips lingering on hers. 'He is my son, *chérie*,' he told her softly. 'And no Frenchman would ever do that to another.' His smile caressed her. 'We shall have our night, I promise you.'

And so, with joy, tenderness and a sweet and soaring passion, they did.

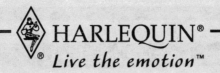

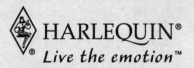

# HARLEQUIN®
# INTRIGUE®

## BREATHTAKING ROMANTIC SUSPENSE

Shared dangers and passions lead to electrifying romance and heart-stopping suspense!

Every month, you'll meet six new heroes who are guaranteed to make your spine tingle and your pulse pound. With them you'll enter into the exciting world of Harlequin Intrigue— where your life is on the line and so is your heart!

## THAT'S INTRIGUE— ROMANTIC SUSPENSE AT ITS BEST!

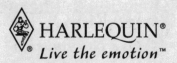

# HARLEQUIN®
*Live the emotion*™

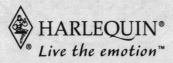

## Harlequin® Historical
### Historical Romantic Adventure!

*Imagine a time of chivalrous knights and unconventional ladies, roguish rakes and impetuous heiresses, rugged cowboys and spirited frontierswomen— these rich and vivid tales will capture your imagination!*

*Harlequin Historical . . . they're too good to miss!*